MAT(

MURDER

Detective Chief Inspector Jon Kim

R. A. JORDAN

This book is dedicated to my grandsons Sam and Dan, and their mother Vanessa, who has worked as editor on some of my books. Her dedication and hard work are very much appreciated.

NHS CHARITIES TOGETHER

I finished writing this book on the 23rd March 2021, the anniversary of the 'lockdown' for the coronavirus pandemic. I intend giving away a number of books, and also selling the majority, with the request the reader makes a donation to NHS CHARITIES TOGETHER in recognition of the exceptional work done by all staff at the NHS during the pandemic.

Donations may be made via my website www.rajordan.uk.

All proceeds donated will be sent to the

NHS CHARITIES TOGETHER

Thank you for your donation.

Rajordan,

In aid of

NHS CHARITIES
TOGETHER

Registered Charity N 1186569

"Murder is a serious business."

Francis Iles

Author of 'Malice Aforethought'

OTHER BOOKS BY R A JORDAN

Time's Up
England's Wall
Laundry
Cracks in the Wall
Secret Side
A Family Lie

To be published shortly:
A Tower of Strength

BOOK REVIEWS

TIME'S UP:

'The writing is excellent, the plot clever.' 'Five star great read.' 'Starts with a bang and will keep you up all night.' 'Great prose, great characters, a cracking plot.'

ENDLAND'S WALL:

'The characters are realistic, like people you know yourself.' 'I don't normally read novels, but this one kept me interested from start to finish. Looks like I will have to read the next one.'

CRACKS IN THE WALL:

'Engaging novel.' 'The way intrigue builds through the novel is really something.'

SECRET SIDE:

'This is a pacey novel with more than its fair share of intrigue, underhand dealings. Murder and suspense.'

The comments are from readers who posted their comments on Amazon. The full versions can be read on my website www.rajordan.uk.

CONTENTS

1

Even before the Premiership football division was formed, derby matches were famous. None more so than the duel between Manchester City and Manchester United. This year the duel was early spring, the middle of March. The anticipation in both camps was intense. Nothing else seemed to be the subject of conversation in the city for the week before the Saturday match.

Jon Kim, a senior detective with Greater Manchester Police and holding a similar position with Cheshire Police, was an ardent Manchester United supporter.

This Friday afternoon he is sitting in his office chatting to his assistant DS Perkins, sweeping up some last-minute details on a case.

Perkins asked Kim the question that had been troubling him for some time.

"I hope you don't mind, sir, but I have been dying to ask you how it is that you work for GMP and Cheshire Police Forces?" Perkins was a thirty-something police officer and, in Kim's reckoning, a good detective. He wasn't a tall man, five-ten or thereabouts. He always wore a stylish suit and tie, with polished shoes. Kim liked that.

"Well, Perkins, don't feel embarrassed. I am happy to fill the gaps in your knowledge."

"Thank you, sir."

"It seems like many years ago now when the British ceded Hong Kong to China. It was the 1st of July 1997. I recall the final day very well. The then-governor, now Lord Patten, welcomed Prince Charles as the representative of the queen to the handover ceremony. He had arrived on HMS *Britannia*, the Royal Yacht. The ship had also brought a contingent of the Royal Marines and their band. The formal handover took place in the evening. It was hot and sticky, with just a breath of wind.

"The military band played the retreat and then the national anthem of the UK. A contingent of the Hong Kong Police took down the Union Jack flag and replaced it with Hong Kong's flag.

"Then there were handshakes with the Chinese representatives, Prince Charles and Lord Patten boarded *Britannia*, followed by the Royal Marines.

After formalities of leaving the dock were completed, this symbol of Britain sailed away down the harbour to sirens and horns; it was a very emotional moment. I was standing with the Royal Hong Kong Police Force contingent to be renamed the following day without the 'Royal' prefix. The heat must have affected some of us as the odd tear was shed, even by hardened police officers."

"I can imagine the scene, sir. It must have been emotional?"

"It was, Perkins, a day I will never forget."

"So what happened next, sir, for you to come to England?"

Kim poured himself another cup of black coffee from the machine, running the events of 1997 over in his head.

"The British, grateful for the help of many Hong Kong public servants, were allowed to apply for British passports if you were deemed eligible. You had to apply; not everyone did. I had no dependents or living relatives. I have always been a supporter of Manchester United. I watched every game as the video was shown on a large screen in the Red Devils pub. It was a supporters' club for Manchester United over the huge souvenir shop for Hong Kong. That's another story.

"The chance of living in England and watching the matches in person was an opportunity too good to miss. I was a detective inspector in the Hong Kong Police, so it was relatively easy for me to get a job with the London Metropolitan Police. After a year or two with the Met, an opportunity arose for me to join Cheshire Police, which I took. It is much nearer to Old Trafford."

"That is very interesting, sir, but how do you get to work for both forces, Cheshire and Manchester?"

"Well, Perkins, I am not married, and my life has been policing. When I achieved the age of fifty-six, I was required to retire, as you may know. I didn't want to retire. I am sure I have many more good years in me yet. However, the constraints on recruitment and budgets meant that the force insisted I left at the time of my birthday. I suggested I could go part-time. There was no specific government direction on part-time work. To ensure I could effectively work full-time, Cheshire's CC spoke with his counterpart in Greater Manchester and hatched a plan. I would work part-time for both forces, with a limited workload for each force."

"I see, sir, that is very imaginative."

"Yes, I was very grateful to both forces. I live in Frodsham near the M56 motorway, so it is reasonably easy to get to both centres when required. It is also easy to get to see Manchester United for a match. However, as it happens, I am staying overnight at the Imperial Hotel near the ground, as I am off to the match tomorrow."

"Thank you, sir. That was most interesting, and I suspect unique in policing?"

"Possibly, Perkins. Are you on duty tomorrow?"

"Yes, I am."

"I hope you have a quiet day."

The two parted company, not expecting what would occur in the next twenty-four hours.

2

Jon Kim left GMP headquarters, having collected his coat and car keys.

His new dark red Jaguar saloon was in the police car park. Less than a thousand miles on the clock, it was Jon Kim's pride and joy. He just loved the smell of the leather, the engine's noise; everything about this car made him feel proud. He drove his new Jaguar car to the Imperial Hotel. Parking up in their basement car park, he knew he would not need to touch it until Sunday morning. The hotel was a short tram journey around the dock to Old Trafford. An easy way to get to the match.

Hotel reception areas differ so much from one to another. At this hotel, a five-star establishment, he was undoubtedly in an upmarket hotel. The floor was marble with Persian rugs. A long reception counter filled one side of this large area. Opposite the entrance doors was a bank of four lifts. Once the formalities had been completed, he was escorted to his room by the bellhop, who insisted on carrying his overnight bag.

Once checked into his room, having parted with a pound coin to the bellhop, he checked out the facilities. There was far more than he required for a one-night stay. Two large wardrobes would never be used. The large king-sized double bed would be more than adequate. The view was over the piazza, with the shopping centre and restaurants opposite. The Lowry theatre was to the left, the Imperial War Museum North to the right.

They said it had a central location, and insofar as this was Salford Quays, it certainly did have a central location. Jon decided some fresh air and a walk would be advantageous. As the Imperial War Museum North was next door, he decided to visit it. Somewhere he had always promised himself to visit. Jon found the whole visit educational and incredibly moving. It was interesting to see exhibits on recent conflicts, Bosnia-Croatia and the missile crisis between the USA and Russia with the missiles destined to be established by Russia in Cuba.

On leaving the museum, he returned to the Imperial Hotel. He made sure that he had a table available to him in the restaurant for dinner at eight o'clock.

The dining room was full; so was the hotel. Many of the regular supporters chose to stay as it was easier to park, and it enabled drinks to be taken.

At seven o'clock on Saturday morning, Jon rose and showered in the excellent modern bathroom, changing into some casual clothes. Smart enough for the executive suite at Manchester United but relaxed enough to be comfortable watching the match. Travelling down to the ground floor in one of the opulent lifts, Jon was immediately aware that the lobby was swarming with police officers. Police tape was covering the entrance to the hotel. Jon could see numerous police vehicles outside.

"What's going on?" Jon enquired of a constable.

"I am sorry I can't help you, sir; there has been an incident."

Jon showed his warrant card.

"Oh, sorry, sir, I didn't know…"

"Don't worry, Constable, you couldn't know. Who is leading the investigation at the moment?"

"DS Perkins, sir, just over there."

Jon knew Perkins was one of the detectives on duty, and he had landed a job. Kim asked Perkins from behind his back, "What is all this about?"

"Sorry, I am too busy at the moment to answer questions," said Perkins, not realising who the questioner was. Not until he turned around, that is. "Sorry, sir, I didn't realise it was you."

"Don't worry, Perkins, but what is going on here?"

"If you have a moment, sir, please come with me."

The two police officers returned to the lifts, pressing button 6.

They soon found themselves on the sixth floor in no time. Perkins gave Kim a brief explanation. "It's a murder; I am sure, sir."

Once out of the lift into the wide corridor, it was not difficult to determine where the 'incident' had occurred. A PCSO was at the door of Room 608 with a clipboard noting comings and goings.

Perkins was acknowledged; Jon Kim showed his warrant card.

Entering the room, a carbon copy of the space he was occupying, Jon had no problem working out what had occurred. There was a man slumped forwards onto the desk. His head was turned away which made it challenging to see who he might be. Blood had trickled down onto the desk and the floor. A Mont-Blanc fountain pen was on the floor nearest to Jon. He knew that the black pen with the trademark white tip could only be that make. Two glasses and a partially empty bottle of vodka, and an opened tin of Coke were on the coffee table, which was in the centre of the space between the double bed and the desk.

"Do you know who the victim is, Perkins?"

"We think so, sir. His jacket was on the bed. According to his wallet and diary, he is or should I say was Graham Phillips. He lived in Alderley Edge."

"Any clues as to how, or who might be responsible for his death?"

"Well, sir, I am still waiting for the pathologist, but I am sure he was stabbed, sir."

"Okay, well, it seems he was left-handed. The document he was signing or writing has disappeared. The knife must have a very long blade."

"How do you know all that, sir? You have only just arrived; do you know him?"

"No, I don't know him. The pen on the floor has the nib exposed and the top placed on the pen's top. As it is on the floor on his left side, I suspect he had been writing on something just before being stabbed."

"I get your point, sir."

"The knife must have had a long blade as he was stabbed through the chair. That would have required two things, a long blade and a drug to anaesthetise the man so he wouldn't move during the stabbing."

"Thank you, sir, that is a real help."

"Look, Perkins, I am staying here tonight. When I check out in the morning, we should go to Alderley Edge and give Mrs Phillips the bad news. Shall we say nine-thirty?"

They agreed. Jon went for breakfast; he arranged with the hotel to stay a further night. They apologised for the inconvenience the police were causing. Jon smiled to himself. No need to explain, but if it were not for the derby match, he would have got stuck in today, and he would do the apologising.

*

Jon was always early for the match. He enjoyed meeting fellow supporters and the friends he had made who sat either side of him in the executive suite seating. The executive area was an area of more comfortable seats in the front of the executive dining room and bar. Jon's seat was one seat in from the aisle.

Jon was in his seat half an hour before the whistle.

The ground would be at capacity today, he mused to himself as he watched each club's supporters take their allocated seats. They say the ground holds seventy-five thousand; it was quite a sight.

Jon had no companions for the first quarter of an hour. The first to arrive was not who he had expected. Gregory Pike was the man who had the aisle seat. Not today. A man he had never met.

"Hello, I'm Jon Kim, pleased to meet you. No Gregory today?"

"No," said the man, engrossed in his mobile phone. "Gregory had a family wedding, so he gave me his ticket."

"You couldn't have got a ticket for a better match."

There was no further response from the man.

"What do I call you?" enquired Kim.

"I am Paul Moore," was the reply, as he continued to maintain a detailed investigation of pages on his mobile phone and answered some by email or text. Jon couldn't help but notice what Paul Moore was doing as he was not someone with whom he could easily converse. Then another man, Julian Hargrave, stood in the aisle waiting for Paul Moore to see he was trying to get past to go to his seat next to Jon.

Once seated, Jon greeted Julian. They conversed about nothing except to speculate on the game; however, Jon was delighted his chum had arrived. The whistle blew; the match started. The teams were so evenly matched it soon became a game of equals. Jon, engrossed in the game, had not realised Paul Moore had gone. No loss there, he thought. He now had more leg room.

*

"What was the match like, sir?"

"Disappointing, Perkins, a one-all draw. Any further news on the murder?"

"No, sir, except the pathologist seemed to think the murder was committed between three and six yesterday afternoon."

"Have you the address for the Phillips' house?" Jon put the postcode coordinates into his satnav, and the pair left for Alderley Edge in Jon's Jaguar.

Chatting in the car, Jon told Perkins that his usual neighbours at the football were the same people who sat in the same seats in the executive area for every match. Yesterday was an exception.

"A chap called Paul Moore sat on my right. I have never seen him before. He didn't say much. He spent most of the time on his mobile and left his seat just after kick-off, not to return.

"Is this the Phillips' house do you think, Perkins?"

Checking the address on his clipboard, Perkins agreed it must be.

The two men approached the front door with a degree of trepidation; it was never easy giving tragic news, especially to a widow.

Kim rang the doorbell.

After a few moments, the front door opened.

It was a man about sixty-eight to seventy, Jon Kim thought. Jon was a little hesitant with his first question, which would be different from the question he had rehearsed.

"Mr Graham Phillips?" enquired Jon Kim.

"Yes, who wants to know?"

"Well, sir," proffering his warrant card as he was answering, "I am DCI Jon Kim of Greater Manchester Police. This is my colleague DS Perkins. We need to speak to you, sir, may we come in?"

Phillips's house was a large Edwardian villa, perched on the side of the escarpment which made Alderley Edge. The view to the west from Phillips's house over towards the Welsh hills was truly magnificent. The two detectives were invited into the lounge.

"I apologise if we seemed incredulous at you answering the door, sir. The issue is that we have found your jacket, wallet, diary and a small amount of cash and credit cards in a room in the Imperial Hotel in Manchester," explained Jon Kim.

"Good heavens, that was quick work. Have you brought my possessions with you?"

"No, sir," replied Kim. "We cannot take credit for the swift discovery of your jacket. Truth to tell, we were drawn to the room where the jacket was found because the room's occupier had been murdered. We thought it was you, sir."

"In that case, Inspector, I understand your surprise when I answered the door. If there is anything I can do to help, you can be assured of my cooperation."

"Thank you, sir."

The two policemen met Mrs Phillips, who put her head around the lounge door; the two officers declined her offer of a cup of tea.

"I need to know your movements on Friday, sir, in particular, where your jacket was first noticed to be missing."

"That is easy." Phillips began the day's story, which mainly included attending a company golf match at a commercial golf course near Knutsford. "I first noticed my jacket was missing after my round of golf when after six hours, I went to the locker room to change."

"On realising your jacket and its contents were gone, what did you do then?"

"I went to find the club manager. He had gone home, so I requested the bar steward accompany me to the locker room. He witnessed that my jacket was not there. He accepted my assertion the locker door was open when I arrived at the locker. I had the key, so I didn't expect the locker to be open. I was staggered when the steward told me that most keys fit most lockers!"

"Are you saying, sir, that any key could have opened your locker?"

"Yes, that is what the steward told me," said Phillips. "Changes will be made to the locks, I assure you, as my company owns this golf club."

"What does trouble me, sir, is how did you drive home when your car keys would be in your jacket, which had by that time had been stolen?"

"Well, Inspector, I never leave my keys in the locker or my jacket. The simple reason being that I need to get my clubs and trolley out of my car once I have changed in the locker room. The reverse is the case after golf. I always keep my car keys with me in my golf bag. My house keys are on my car keys."

"Thank you, sir, that clears that query up very well. I guess we will be paying a visit to the golf club," advised Kim. "However, who was running the golf day?"

"That's easy. It was Tudor Wainwright, a firm of Chartered Surveyors in Manchester. I used to be a Chartered Surveyor until I retired."

"Who did you work for, sir?"

"I worked for myself. My firm was a large surveying practice which I sold about ten years ago now."

"Did you carry on working following the sale, sir?"

"Yes, Inspector, but not as a Charted Surveyor. The agreement on my company's sale barred me from working as a Surveyor unless I moved away. No, I started a small finance and mortgage company, specialising in residential and commercial investment properties."

"I see, sir. Well, there is not a great deal more we need at the moment, sir. If we need to talk to you again, we will be in contact."

"Inspector, when will I get my possessions back? It's the diary I need more than anything."

"I am afraid the jacket, and all its contents will be required as evidence. Just one thing, what sort of pen did you use?"

"I now use, or did, a Mont Blanc pen. A present from my staff when I sold the business. They all received a bonus on the sale."

"Thank you, sir; that's all we need for now."

Jon Kim and Perkins left Phillips' house, with a smile on their faces as they had received so much information which was guaranteed correct, as far as the two policemen could ascertain.

"We have a problem now, Perkins. Who is the dead man?"

"I agree, sir; we need to start again."

"Best if you go to go to this golf club, Perkins."

"I doubt the manager of the club will be there on a Sunday, sir," suggested Perkins.

Jon phoned GMP HQ on his mobile phone, which had a Bluetooth connection to the car's electronic system. The call was then 'hands-free' and he asked them to determine if the manager was at the golf club.

"Sir, it's GMP; no, the manager will be at the club sometime after ten tomorrow morning."

"Well, that's that. Not much more we can do today. Perkins, I will drop you off at HQ and see you tomorrow."

As Jon realised it was not out of his way, driving home to Frodsham to visit the golf club near Knutsford could be achieved quickly without too much of a diversion. He thought he would call in.

Driving through the golf course, Jon obeyed the signs about flying golf balls, stopping at intervals to ensure his new car would not be hit by a ball.

Sunday is always a busy day at golf clubs; this one was no exception. The car park was full, so Jon parked in the space reserved for the manager, who he had established would not be in today. He received a few quizzical glances from members, but no one questioned him.

"Is the steward available?" Jon inquired of the man behind the bar.

"I am the steward, sir; how can I help you?"

"I am a police officer with GMP. Were you on duty last Friday?"

"Yes, sir, is this about the missing jacket?"

"It is."

"Well, the owner must have friends in high places. We were unable to get anyone to come out when there was a burglary at the club."

"It's a little more complicated than that. However, could you please show me the locker that was robbed?"

"Follow me, sir. I can't spend too long as I am on my own this afternoon. The golfers will soon start to come in for afternoon tea or something stronger."

"I understand. Thank you for taking the time."

"This is the locker, sir."

Jon looked at the space behind the narrow door. There was one shelf and two hooks inside. The key was in the door. Jon removed the key and tried to unlock the adjoining locker. It opened. It was full of clothes. He locked it again.

"I was told the keys would fit any locker. The security is not very good."

"There is a sign over there, sir, warning players not to leave valuables in the lockers."

"I am not sure that would be sufficient if someone took the club to court. If you provide lockers with keys, the key should be unique to the locker. It's very gloomy here. Do you always have the lighting this low?"

"Yes, sir, I am told it aids privacy; I agree, sir. I will mention the keys and lighting to the manager."

"What's his name?"

"Major Ives, sir."

"Would he be able to tell me who came to play on Friday?"

"He might, but as it was a society day, the organisers can invite people, so we will not know them unless they are members of this club."

"Thanks; what's your name?"

"Mike, sir. Everyone knows me as Mike."

"What is your last name?"

"Fry, sir."

"Thank you, Mike. I will let you get on with your duties. I may be back tomorrow."

3

The county of Shropshire, bordered by Wales, has rolling countryside, without the interference of a large town or city. In Victorian times, the countryside's attractiveness had persuaded several boarding schools for boys and girls to be constructed in the county.

Grange Hall School was just one of many such schools. Standing within magnificent grounds, it was no longer the exclusive domain of boys. Girls had been admitted some years earlier into the sixth form college.

New 'houses' had been constructed over the years as boys' requirement to be privately educated increased. The latest of these houses was the girls' house.

The girls' house created the final side of the quadrangle. Formed by the Old Hall, two new boys' houses had been provided, one to the north, the other to the quadrangle's south side. The new girls' house closed the 'quad' on the westerly side. Once the development was completed, there were six houses in all. There were three forming a 'quad' – with the Hall on the other side, the East Quad. The girls' house made up the three in the West Quad. The total complement of the school was one hundred and eighty children. Thirty in each 'house'. There was a housemaster to each of the boys' houses, who lived in the house. A housemistress in the girls' house.

The headmaster was delighted he had persuaded so many overseas students to come to Grange Hall. The chatter and banter in the quads was uncanny. It was an international babble of young voices in so many different languages. Chinese was in the majority. Grange Hall had achieved an enviable reputation. Children from the armed forces, children of business people, and international students, plus most British students. All students had to pass their common entrance examination to be permitted to attend the school.

As it was Saturday, and the thought of home exaggerated an exeat weekend, the anticipation in school was of comfy beds and Mum's home cooking. There would be a cavalcade of four-by-four cars of all types, but predominantly Range Rovers, arriving at the school to collect the children.

"Paul, I am going to collect Richard from school. You are off to the match I gather?"

"Yes, I will need to get going as noon is the latest to get a parking slot. Greg Pike gave me his executive ticket as he has a family wedding to go to."

"I will be bringing Richard and Bao from school. His parents are in China; the overseas pupils remain at school on exeats if they are not invited home by a pupil. Richard thought it would be good for him to come to us for the weekend."

"Good for Richard. Have a good trip, don't drive too quickly, it's a new car, and even though manufacturers don't require cars to be 'run-in', I think it is good for the car. See you later, Di."

Paul's BMW left the family home in Wilmslow first. Diana was not far behind. She had a good hour and a half to go to get to Grange Hall School.

Diana enjoyed her first long trip in her new Range Rover; she felt she had now arrived with this top-of-the-range-car. She couldn't wait until the next lunch date to show off to her friends this new car. They would all be jealous, she hoped.

Within an hour and twenty minutes, she arrived at Grange Hall School. Parents were waiting in the access road to the school for their charges to be released. It was twelve-thirty on the dot when Bao appeared, looking to find Richard's parents' car.

"Bao, I am here," announced Diana Moore, waving like mad from the open car window.

"Hello, Mrs Moore," Bao said in a perfect English accent with Chinese overtones.

Di was impressed by this boy who arrived on time, smartly dressed in polished shoes and his weekend bag.

"Let's pop your bag in the boot; you hop in the front, Bao; you have earned a trip in the front as you are first here."

Ten minutes later, Richard appeared.

"Just look at you."

"Hello Mum, is Bao here?"

"Yes, he is in the front."

"Oh, I wanted to sit there."

"Well, you can on the way back. You are ten minutes behind most other students who are on their way home now. Just look at you, muddy shoes, a scruffy tie and jacket. When did you last brush your hair? I don't know, Richard, you need to take some lessons from Bao."

"Can I sit in the middle, Mum, so that I can see the dials?"

"Okay, in you get, keep your feet off the seats, and put your seat belt on."

Richard did as he was told up to a point. He sat in the middle seat, so he had a clear view ahead. He could see the dials, which pleased him greatly. He enjoyed touching all the buttons located at the back of the central arm rest. Aircon was one, a cigar lighter and reading light controls were all available.

"The seats are lovely, Mum, very comfy; there are a lot of buttons in the back, Mum."

Di drove out of Grange Hall School setting her destination as her home in Wilmslow. The M56 motorway was reasonably straightforward. The derby football match between City and United in Manchester ensured that most supporters would have arrived in time to enjoy a pint and a pie before the game.

"How fast will it go, Mum?" enquired Richard from the back seat, scanning the dials in front of his mother.

"Have you still got your seat belt on, Richard?"

"Yes, Mum."

"Why are boys so fascinated with speed?" Diana muttered to herself as she eased the car up to eighty miles an hour.

"Go on, Mum, these cars will go much faster than that."

Eighty-five, ninety, ninety-three, ninety-five.

"That's fast enough, Richard; I have to slow down now as we shall be turning off soon."

As Di took the junction signposted for Wilmslow and Altrincham, she could see that major road works were still in operation, despite it being a Saturday. The new access and improved roads around the junction were designed to give an extensive new industrial estate access. Just after you make your way to the exit for Wilmslow, there were coned-off single-track carriageways.

Once free of the works, which included a substantial new Amazon warehouse, the road became a dual carriageway as the twin tunnels under the Manchester Airport runways came into sight. Di could see ahead was a massive lorry. She put her foot down, knowing there a twisty road after the tunnels into Wilmslow; the lorry would cause her to be held up.

"Go on, Mum, you can easily get past that," encouraged Richard from the back seat. He had removed his seat belt to sit with his body between the front seats and watch the dials as the speed increased over seventy, maybe more.

As Di approached the Polish lorry's rear, it moved over to the outside lane to overtake a slow car. The lorry, partway through its manoeuvre, formed a triangle with no route through for Di. Being a new car, she pressed what she was sure was the brake but hit the accelerator by mistake. The Range Rover gave an extra spurt of speed until Di, in a split second, realised she would have a crash and hit the other pedal. The brake.

She was terrified she was going to crash.

"Oh no!" she shouted. There was nowhere to go. The lorry was unaware of the impending crash, the driver sitting high up and on the left-hand side as it was a foreign vehicle which continued to close the gap.

The Range Rover was squeezed tight up against the concrete wall of the tunnel. The sound was deafening, screeching metal on concrete – a magnified version of a teacher's nails on a blackboard.

The loud noise of the two different-sized vehicles' impact must have been heard well back in the queue of cars coming along behind. Vehicles began to display their hazard lights immediately. The Range Rover was now sandwiched between the concrete wall of the tunnel and the massive lorry. Despite its size, the Range Rover was severely squashed.

In the Range Rover, the airbag safety system had been activated with a bang, showering the inside of the car with a white powder. Richard had been caught by the inertia the car had created; from eighty miles an hour to a complete stop in hardly any distance. A force of nature Richard could not overcome. He was thrown forward, not being constrained by his seat belt, crashing headfirst into the windscreen.

There was a strange moment of silence. Then a voice was heard from a man who had run from his car. He was shouting into his mobile phone.

"I am an off-duty sergeant, C362. Eastbound tunnel under the airport large RTC two ambulances and paramedic doctor, fire appliance, and many more officers urgently required."

This professional call gave all the information the police control room needed to put into action a significant response to the incident.

The first on the scene was a paramedic car followed by an ambulance, and another ambulance. The fire service were only minutes behind them. The issue was that they all arrived from the Wilmslow direction and needed to change carriageways, which they did by crossing the central reservation at the commencement of the tunnels.

A senior traffic inspector arrived in an unmarked BMW with blue lights flashing from their discreet locations around the car. He took immediate charge, getting traffic in the queue turned around, sending them back to the M56. He had officers placed at the junction with the M56, stopping any further traffic from joining the already congested area.

The paramedic made an initial assessment of the Range Rover passengers, realising that a boy was dead, having hit the windscreen very hard. So the casualties could be extracted, the lorry needed to be moved. A senior police officer and a member of the ambulance crew took the lorry driver from his cab. The ambulance paramedic promised to dress his head wound. The police officer managed to reverse the lorry sufficiently so the Range Rover could be accessed.

Diana Moore was seriously injured. Her side of the car had taken the full impact of the concrete wall.

An announcement was made at the Manchester United and City derby match at half time. It warned drivers that the junction off the M56 to Wilmslow and Altrincham was blocked due to an incident. It would remain blocked for most of the rest of the day.

Di was taken to the primary trauma unit at Wythenshawe Hospital, with Bao in the second ambulance. He had two broken legs and bruising. He was sent to the same hospital.

A family liaison officer managed to discover the name of the driver, Diana Moore. She also found the mobile phone number of her husband from her diary.

A phone call to Paul Moore found him in the crowd at Old Trafford. The background noise was deafening. He promised to go to Wythenshawe Hospital straight away.

Moore nodded to Jon Kim and left the ground shortly after the start of the match. He didn't return.

4

Jon Kim returned on Monday morning to GMP headquarters to restart the investigation into the anonymous man in room 608.

"Perkins, have you asked for a photo of the murdered man from the pathologist?"

"Yes, sir, it is due later today."

"Okay. Are you off to the golf club? I am going to do some desk research into Graham Phillips as he was certainly the intended victim. It looks like I will have a day of staring at a screen as I try and unravel elements of this case."

*

"Is that the manager of the Imperial Hotel? DCI Jon Kim, Greater Manchester Police here. I am sure my SOCO team will have taken some of the CCTV footage you have, but I wonder if you might have some footage they have not requested? I am trying to spot someone who I don't know. I want to look at the comings and goings through reception. Ideally from noon on Friday to about five in the afternoon."

"I can do that for you, sir. Let me have your email address, sir; I will send you the footage within the hour."

True to his word, the manager sent the footage to Jon, who then spent the remaining morning scanning the footage.

"God, this is boring," Jon muttered to himself. "Sorry to bother you again," Jon said to the Imperial's manager. "Can you tell me the time the occupant of room 608 checked in and what name he used?"

"Yes, sir. It was at two forty-five on Friday. He checked in as Graham Phillips."

"You are very efficient. I can tell you the man who took the room is not Graham Phillips. While I have you on the phone, do you recall Mr Phillips phoning to say he would not be staying the night? I guess that would be sometime between three and four p.m. On Friday."

"He didn't speak to me, sir, but if he spoke to one of my reception staff, they would have seen the room had already been re-let, so there was no issue or charge for Mr Phillips."

"Okay, I get it, thanks."

Jon returned to his computer and began watching the footage from half past two on Friday afternoon.

There was a knock on the door, and a young lady came in with an envelope.

"DCI Kim?" she asked.

"Yes."

"I have an envelope for you from Pathology."

"Thanks." Jon was impatient to open the envelope, ripping the tab off the top, extracting the photo.

"Whoa!" Jon exclaimed to himself in his office, which was devoid of all staff. He couldn't believe his eyes.

"How on God's earth could this be Paul Moore?" Jon knew immediately who this person was; Jon knew the man in the photograph had been murdered on Friday afternoon. "So, who the hell is this?" It couldn't be Paul Moore, as he was sitting, for a short time, next to Jon at the match.

He continued his search of the CCTV footage of the reception area. At ten minutes to three, the man who had his back to the camera turned around, holding a key card and papers. The focus was blurred, so it was not possible to identify the man's features.

The man had a small holdall in his other hand. He was wearing a checked jacket. He walked to the lifts. Jon was sure it was the man in the photograph.

Jon's next call was to the firm of Tudor Wainwright. Once he was put through to the individual who had organised the golf day, Jon hoped to discover if there was a list of attendees with contact details.

"Mr Kim, my secretary tells me you are from the police? I am Justin Lois, a partner of the firm and main organiser of the golf day. My secretary has placed on my desk a list of our attendees and their contact details. The issue I have is one of data protection. We don't hand out details of our attendees to anyone."

"Well, sir, I am not sure you are fully aware of who I am. I am a DCI with Greater Manchester Police. I am investigating a murder and the theft of a jacket from one of your attendees. The jacket was recovered from the murder scene."

"Oh, dear me. That does throw a different light on the matter. I suppose the police have powers to request the data?"

"We do, but there is a process to go through. I would far rather we had an understanding. I will only try and find one or two people that could be helpful in our enquiries. I can assure you the list will be held securely."

"Mr Kim, I will not stand in your way. It would be best if you caught the culprit. I hope the murderer is not on my list. If you give me your email address, I will send the list to you immediately."

Within minutes of putting the phone down, Jon had the list he required. Perusing the names, he spotted Paul Moore. The man who sat next to Jon at the football. Would there be anyone at home? He tried but got no reply.

"Mr Lois, sorry to bother you again. Would you by chance happen to know what business Mr Paul Moore has?"

"Yes, he is a commercial jeweller. His premises are on Dale Street in Manchester."

"Out of interest, how do you know that?"

"We manage the property on behalf of the landlord."

Jon then phoned Manchester United and let them understand who he was and why he needed some information. In the end, he was put through to the manager of the membership subscriptions. Once again, Jon was faced with a data protection argument. Eventually, he persuaded the manager to reveal the information on Gregory Pike, Jon's neighbour in the executive suite.

"Thank you," said Jon once the data he required was made available to him.

Eventually, Jon was able to speak with Gregory Pike. Jon realised it had taken him an hour to make this call.

"Gregory, I am Jon Kim. I sit next to you in the executive seating at Manchester United. Sorry to have missed you this weekend."

"Hi, Jon. Yes, I had a family wedding to attend."

"Well, I am investigating a serious crime. The person who sat in your seat could be of interest to me."

"Paul Moore?"

"Yes, that's the man. Can you tell me what you know about him and how he came to have your ticket?"

"Easy, I have known Paul for years. He is a commercial jeweller in Manchester. He has sold me the odd gem for my wife. Our children go to the same school. I met him at a golf day near Knutsford on Friday. I had my ticket in my pocket and gave it to Paul as I couldn't go. He was delighted."

"Okay, thanks. Do you have the address for Paul Moore's business?"

"Yes, I do. Let me email it to you. I know it's on Dale Street, but I cannot recall the number. Could you give me your email?"

Jon reflected on the internet's magic. Within two hours of starting his investigation, he had all the required information.

Jon took his car to Dale Street and parked on yellow lines, with his police notice left in the window, to put off keen parking attendants.

The property was not a shop; why Jon should imagine it would be, he didn't know. The premises were a two-storey red-brick Victorian building. "It probably started life as a house," Jon muttered to himself. The window frames had not been painted in decades. The front door was robust but, again, in need of paint. Next door was a similar property. Further down the street a building had been demolished so the site could be used as a car park.

Jon rang the bell. The bell then spoke to him. "Who are you, and what do you want?"

"I am DCI Jon Kim of GMP. May I come in and speak with you?"

"Please show your warrant card to the camera in the bell push."

Jon did as requested, and the door made a buzzing noise, allowing him to push the door open.

Jon didn't get far, just into a lobby, with another camera, another area that needed painting.

"Please push the front door shut; then I will open the second door for you."

Jon did as he was asked. The second door opened into a Dickensian property. It was a gloomy space, with a narrow corridor leading to a further door, which was ajar. He made his way to the back of the premises. The decorations were worse inside than out. This place had not seen a lick of paint for decades. Nicotine staining on walls and ceilings. Wallpaper hanging off in a corner where there was a clear indication of damp. There was a damp smell and an unknown metallic odour, which permeated the air.

Jon muttered that if Mr Lois was the managing agent, he should get around here and fix the place.

"Mr Kim, I am sorry for the maze to get you in. As jewellers, we must be careful, so we are not raided. If I have doubts, I leave the visitor in the inner lobby until I am satisfied."

Jon was looking at an older man in his late sixties. Grey hair but plenty of it. He wore a white shirt without a collar with the top button undone, under a black waistcoat with black trousers. The ensemble was completed by round tortoiseshell spectacles and black shoes, more like boots, that needed cleaning.

"Very sensible. Who are you?"

"Oh, sorry, I am Joseph White, the manager, well, the only employee at the moment of Moore's jewellers."

"Can I call you, Joseph? Please call me Jon." Jon opened the conversation with a smile on his face. He was confident he would be able to learn a great deal from this man.

"Jon, please sit down, yes, use the chair at that desk. It's Mr Paul's, but he will not be in today or this week. This is my desk."

"Oh, why is that?"

"His wife has had a serious car accident. Their son was killed. He is distraught."

"Yes, I am sure. How did you discover that?"

"Oh, Mr Paul very unusually rang me after lunch on Saturday to tell me and that he would not be around for a while."

"Do you know what time exactly he called you?"

"It would be about three in the afternoon. I was about to watch the match."

"So was I, Joseph. I was there."

"It wasn't worth watching in the end. Well, that's what I think, Jon."

"This place looks very intriguing. Those benches and stools with Anglepoise lights over the desk and large magnifying glasses on adjustable stems; what's all that about?"

"Well, Jon, we are commercial jewellers. We used to purchase precious stones from Antwerp's gem dealers. Mr Paul's grandfather started that. You know, diamonds, emeralds, rubies and so on, set them in rings, brooches, and other jewellery. Whatever the retail jeweller ordered. We also repaired jewellery on behalf of retail jewellers."

"Quite a business. You say, 'used to', Joseph. Don't you do that anymore?"

"No, regrettably. Paul's father then carried on the business founded by Paul's grandfather. Since Paul inherited the business, he has not done very well. He got rid of the talented jewellers, who would sit at those benches all day long and make the most amazing items.

It's a great shame because we have lost the connections with most of our jewellers who used to send us a great deal of work and order wonderful gems."

"Oh, so what happens now?" enquired Jon.

"Well, we still purchase items from Antwerp, ready-made items. We don't do any manufacture or repairs. Short-sighted as the repair business was very lucrative."

"I see. So, Paul sells the gems on to the retail trade?"

"Yes, that's it. There is not much of a markup. Most jewellery retailers are buying stuff far cheaper from the Indians, without coming to us. The Indians don't do repairs or make anything unique, so our connection with many retailers has gone. I don't see the firm lasting all that long."

"Is the company in financial difficulty, Joseph?"

"I shouldn't say, sir."

"Do you live far away, Joseph?"

"No, not at all. I live in the flat upstairs. Paul doesn't pay me much; he cannot afford to, not with the amount of money he takes out of the business. I don't pay rent, so that is helpful, I suppose."

"Are those files in bright blue the bank statements?"

"Yes, Jon."

"Well, while you make me a cup of coffee, I will have a look at the contents. Then you will be able to say you didn't tell me about the finances truthfully."

Joseph smiled as he got up to make a coffee for Jon and a cup of tea for himself. Jon reached up to pull a couple of binders out to look at bank statements. The notation 'od' against all the balances indicated a significant overdraft.

The company was overdrawn to the tune of over fifty thousand pounds. Money was leaving the bank at an extraordinary rate. There was little in the way of income.

Jon looked carefully at the expenditure. There was a standing order of over a thousand pounds a month to JLR Finance. That is the financial arm of Jaguar Land Rover. Another three thousand a month went to Paul Moore's account. Eight hundred a month went to Joseph White. There were payments for rates and insurance. That was a varying monthly payment to Gregory Pike & Co, insurance brokers. Jon realised there was no rent being paid.

The coffee arrived; Jon returned the files to the shelf.

"The finances certainly look precarious, Joseph."

"Yes, Jon. I can't see it lasting very long."

"The coincidence in all this is that Paul Moore sat next to me at the derby match at Old Trafford on Saturday. He left shortly after the game started. He had several calls on his mobile phone. One must have been to you?"

"Yes, that would make sense. His wife had crashed the new Range Rover; she is in the Wythenshawe hospital."

"That would explain his early departure. I can see rates going out of the account, but no rent. Does Paul own the property?"

"No, I am sure he doesn't. There is a mortgage on it to Aktaion Limited, but I don't know anything about that. The rent we pay goes out quarterly. The next payment is due on March 25th, Lady Day."

"Okay, Joseph, you have been more than helpful. I may see you again; you never know."

5

Paul had discovered that he couldn't go to the hospital until visiting times. He had been told that under no circumstances would he be permitted to enter outside visiting time by an officious administrator on Saturday. He realised he hadn't spoken to the school.

"Hello, it's Paul Moore speaking. Can I talk to Gerry Evans, housemaster to Bishop House, please?

"Gerry, it's Paul Moore. I am so sorry; I have had one hell of a weekend. I should have phoned you yesterday. The issue is that on the way home on Saturday for the exeat weekend, my wife had a massive crash with a large lorry. Richard was killed."

A tear fell down his cheek at the mention of Richard's name.

"Sorry, Gerry, it's painful. The crash has put both my wife and Bao in hospital. He has two broken legs."

"Oh, Paul, how awful. Which hospital is Bao in,

please?"

"Wythenshawe Hospital near Manchester. It's an excellent place." Paul was not processing the content of this conversation.

"Look, Paul, I have to tell the headmaster. I am very sorry for your loss. We may have to get back to you once we have spoken with Bao's parents."

Paul was more troubled today than he was yesterday. He was unable to take in the magnitude of the events of Saturday. What was he to do? He was sorely troubled. Everything was closing in on him; the bank for the firm was seriously overdrawn, the quarterly rent was due in two weeks on the March quarter day. His finances were no better. He began to shake, and a cold sweat made him shiver even more. His future looked bleak.

*

At the golf club near Knutsford, the manager was keen to try and help Perkins.

"One of your officers called in here yesterday and spoke to the steward."

"Yes, that was DCI Jon Kim. He was on his way home and thought he would call in. What I need, sir, is a copy of your membership records. And details of all your staff – stewards, cleaners ground staff and of course you, sir."

"Good grief, why on earth do you need all this information for the loss of a jacket?"

"The lost jacket, sir, has been found. It was in a bedroom in the Imperial Hotel, Manchester, where a man was murdered on Friday evening."

"Oh, I see, not just a straightforward theft. I understand. Well, under data protection regulations, I am certain I should not release this information to you. However, I will as we don't wish to impede the work of the police."

"Thank you, sir. We do have a right to require certain information that might have protection from the Data Protection Act. We would normally have to seek a court order that takes time; in a murder enquiry, time is of the essence."

"I do understand, Sergeant. Can you bear with me while I collate the documents you require? I assume a printout from the computer payroll will be sufficient. It has everyone employed on it, including me, as well as their addresses and phone number."

"Can I ask, sir, is this club owned by its members or is it owned by a company?"

"Unusual question, but you are very astute. It is owned as a profitable venture by an investment and finance company."

"In which case, the name and address of the company, their directors and directors of the golf club will need adding to my request. Will it be okay if I wait in the lounge area?"

"Yes, certainly, please help yourself to a coffee."

While Perkins was having a coffee watching a few members playing on the course, the manager, whose name Perkins had yet to confirm, sat in his office with the printer running. He made a phone call.

"Graham, it's Rupert. I have another policeman here. He is asking for details of the members and the details of the owners of the club."

"Well, give him what he wants. They won't be bright enough to make a connection. Are you okay?"

"Yes, the job is done."

"Yes, well done. You know your reward; it will have to wait until the dust has settled."

"Okay, I will sort this policeman out now; got to go... Sergeant Perkins, I think this is all the information you need."

"Thank you, sir; I forgot to ask your name?"

"Major Rupert Ives. My details are on the sheet."

"Army?" enquired Perkins.

"Yes, in the end, I was in the TA, Cheshire regiment. I have been a civil servant most of my life after leaving Cambridge. The Civil Service seem to like to trawl the corridors of universities."

"That sounds interesting. Did you work in London?"

"Yes, to begin with, then I was posted abroad."

"Foreign office posting?"

"Yes, that sort of thing. All very interesting. Not as peaceful as it is here," said Ives.

"What did your wife say about that?"

"Oh, I have never married. I was too involved with my work."

"Where did the FO send you, sir?" asked Perkins.

"All over. They seemed to find tough areas for me. Probably because I had no family. Iraq, Bosnia, and Russia."

"They sound tough gigs. How did you get on with the languages?"

"No problem. My degree was in modern languages

and the classics. I speak Russian and Arabic. The language in Bosnia and Croatia is not that far from Russian."

"Sounds like a fascinating life."

"It was, but I prefer the job here. Not so dangerous."

"Thank you, sir; I hope we don't have to bother you again."

Perkins returned to GMP HQ for a meeting with his boss.

"Sir, have you a moment. I need to discuss various issues with you that have come to light as a result of my enquiries."

"I bet your information is not a patch on mine," said Jon Kim, grinning from ear to ear.

"Well, sir, let's go through it all. We can then decide who has had the best day."

They were about to commence their meeting when there was a knock on the door.

A SOCO officer held a plastic exhibit bag with what looked like a piece of paper inside.

"Sir, my boss thought you should have this. It was crumpled up in the waste bin in room 608. It might not mean anything; however, you should have it."

The two police officers took the bag and had a close look at both sides of the paper. There was one word, written in blue ink, on one side. The word looked unfinished. The word started with the letters S T A. The last letter was not clear. It hadn't been formed, but it could be a O or S, a G, or a Q. It had the curl on the left, which would match any of these letters. The letters were spaced apart; they could be initials or the start of a word.

"Was the dead man trying to tell us something? Did the victim write these letters, or was it someone else?" asked Kim.

"It's hard to say, sir."

"So, tell me, Perkins, what have you found out at the golf club?"

"Well, I had a good session with the manager of the club, Major Rupert Ives. He was TA with the Cheshire regiment. He had been to Bosnia, Russia, and other hotspots. He was charming and accommodating. He told me the club is owned by a company, which I need to investigate – Aktaion Limited."

"I have received the photo of the dead man from pathology," said Kim. "The fantastic thing is that the man in the photograph, the dead man, sat next to me at Old Trafford's match. That, of course, is impossible. He was declared dead on Saturday morning as having been stabbed on Friday between three and six in the afternoon. The match didn't start until three on Saturday afternoon. Paul Moore sat next to me, having been gifted the ticket by Greg Pike, who had to go to a family wedding."

"Do you think Paul Moore has a twin brother?" suggested Perkins.

Jon had already phoned Joseph, who told Jon that he did have a twin brother.

"Joseph said he is in Finance. He didn't know which firm," confirmed Jon.

"Interesting, that is Graham Phillips' business."

"You are right, Perkins, let me go to Companies House again."

Jon now believed they were on to a rich seam of information, leading to the murderer. Motive was the concern, but indeed money is often the root cause of murder.

Jon put in the details of the company, Aktaion Ltd. The directors were Graham Phillips, Rupert Ives, and Peter Moore.

"Well, there's a bit of information we didn't have before," said Jon. "There is a close connection between these people. I wonder what has gone on. Do you suppose that one or both of the other two directors have wanted Peter Moore removed for some reason?"

"It is likely, sir. What motive could they have?"

"Look, Perkins, you have met Ives, have a look at the CCTV for the hotel's reception on Friday afternoon to see if you can find him. I seem to recall he had left early from the golf club."

Jon contacted SOCO and the forensic department, wanting their report on the crime scene as soon as possible. They promised to email it to him within the hour.

6

It was Tuesday morning. Paul Moore was at home in Wilmslow. He hadn't been able to sleep. He was distraught about his son's death – Diana in hospital and little Bao, with two broken legs.

He had to eat something. The easiest was cereal. He had only a little milk, so he swore as he ate the nearly dry breakfast. Some slightly stale bread would make toast. He needed to pull himself together and do some shopping. Have a shower and generally tidy himself up. What had happened had happened. "What else could go wrong?" he muttered to himself.

Paul had just finished his flakes when the phone rang. He let it ring.

The answerphone sent the pre-recorded message.

Ten minutes later, as he was finishing his toast, the phone rang again.

"Damn," Paul said to himself and answered the phone.

"Mr Paul Moore? I am DCI Kim at Greater Manchester Police."

"I am sorry, I don't think I can help you as I was not in the car, and I only know the implications of the crash."

"It's not about the crash, sir. I want to come and see you. I am a detective from the murder squad."

"Oh, whatever next?"

"Will eleven o'clock this morning be okay?"

"Yes, I suppose so." Paul put the phone down, wondering what on earth the police wanted.

He decided to go to a local shop which the Co-Op had established in a filling station nearby. At least he could park there and be back in time for the police.

Paul arrived back home at ten forty-five, as a dark red Jaguar saloon pulled up outside his house. A small Chinese man got out. Could he be the police?

Realising he must be the police, he struggled with three carrier bags, opening the front door, inviting the two police officers to follow him.

The two police officers showed their warrant cards to Paul as they followed him into the kitchen and then the lounge as soon as Paul had put the milk in the fridge.

Paul invited the policemen to sit down; on this occasion, they sat. Jon felt this could be a lengthy interview. He could tell the house needed some improvement. Wear on carpets and decorations looking tired was all too obvious. Money was his problem despite the money he was taking out of the jewellery business. Jon assumed his wife was spending the money.

"Mr Moore, I am Jon Kim. This is DS Perkins. We are here about your twin brother."

"Oh, what's the matter with Peter?"

"Well, sir, I am sorry to have to tell you that he was murdered on Friday afternoon."

"Oh, no. Why has it taken you so long to tell me? It's Tuesday today."

"Well, sir, the issue has been one of identification. It was only late yesterday. I received a photograph of your brother from pathology. As soon as I saw it, I thought it was you. It couldn't have been you as you sat next to me for a while at Old Trafford for the derby match on Saturday. It took some time to track you down as your ticket belonged to Greg Pike. I didn't have his contact details; data protection had to be overcome to allow me to get them from Manchester United. Greg Pike gave me your number."

"I see, quite a bit of detective work then. So, my twin brother is dead? How did he die, Inspector?"

"Yes, sir. He was stabbed in a room at the Imperial Hotel at Old Trafford. Were you close as twins very often are?"

"No, we were not. There was a massive falling out when my father died. He left the business to me and a small amount of money to Peter. Peter was furious; he thought he could do a much better job running the business than me. He had qualified as an accountant. He worked in a bank, where he graduated to the investment side of the bank. As one politician put it some years ago, the casino banking operation."

"When did you last see your brother?"

"It must be four years ago when he left the bank. I didn't see him. He just rang to say he had a new job as a finance company director and investment business."

"Where did he work, sir?"

"The firm has a Greek name. Something about not infringing the name of other companies with a similar name."

"Would it be Aktaion?"

"Yes, that's the name. I have no idea what he did there. The only other contact I have had with him was when we wanted a re-mortgage on the house. Our son, no, sorry…"

Paul broke down in tears. The realisation that Richard was no longer alive hit Paul hard. He couldn't speak for a while. Kim and Perkins let him get over his breakdown. He sobbed and then cleared his throat, ready to resume.

"I am sorry, sir. Of course, we were aware of the accident. I presumed that is why you left the match soon after it started."

"You are correct, of course. It has been a traumatic few days. What I was about to say was we needed a new mortgage to help pay the school fees for Richard, which are not needed now." Another tear trickled down his cheek, at the realisation the pain of school fees had ended.

"Our visit is not a good time for you, sir. I recognise that. We do, however, need the identification of your brother. Would you be prepared to do that for us?"

"Yes, I suppose it will be the last thing I could do for him. Despite our differences, we are or were brothers."

"Thank you, sir; one more thing, was your brother right- or left-handed?"

"He was left-handed; strangely, I am right-handed."

"Can you please tell us what your movements were on Friday last?"

"I was down to play in a golf match at Knutsford. I was invited by the managing agents of my company's premises, Tudor Wainwright. I left here at about eleven o'clock, having spoken on the phone to Joseph White, he runs the business for me. I played golf, teeing off at twelve-thirty. The round was slow, just under five hours. It would be about five-fifteen when we got back to the clubhouse. I had a sandwich and a drink. After prize-giving, I came home."

"Thank you, sir; an officer will come and collect you and take you to the mortuary. Can you please give us your mobile number? I expect you will be visiting the hospital quite regularly?"

The two detectives thanked Moore for his co-operation and left.

"Right, Perkins," when the two were back in Kim's car, "what we need now is a search warrant to the company premises of Aktaion Limited and their accountants. It looks like they share the same address at Old Trafford. We need a search team and a sniffer dog, in case there are drugs on the premises."

Kim was sure there was a financial aspect to this case. Paul Moore was most in need of cash, but he didn't appear to be the sort of man who would murder his brother. He might have been tempted when their father died, but not four years later. Peter had helped arrange a second mortgage for the school fees. No, I have a feeling there is some other person with a motive.

"Yes, sir, I can fix all that. What time do you think would be appropriate?"

"As they are business premises, we should aim to be there at say, nine-thirty."

*

Paul Moore sorted out his shopping once the police had gone. He realised the day was moving on; he needed to be at the hospital in an hour. As he was trying to get his mind in order with events that had occurred, his mobile rang.

"Mr Moore?"

"Yes, who is this?"

"Wythenshawe Hospital. I am just phoning to advise you that your wife has just gone into theatre;

she has bleeding on the brain."

"Oh, no. What will that mean? When can I come and see her?"

"She will be in the intensive care ward when she is back; you can come whenever you like, sir. She is likely to be away for a couple of hours."

Paul felt like he was underwater and about to drown. It was difficult to breathe and compute the events that had occurred; he thought he was drowning in devastating news.

He decided it could be a long night. A glass of whisky, paracetamol; sleep would be best. Then he could go to the hospital later.

"What the hell?" Paul was woken from his deep sleep by the perpetual ringing of the landline phone.

"Yes," said Paul as he answered the phone.

"It's Wythenshawe Hospital here, sir. Who am I talking to?"

"Paul, Paul Moore. What do you want?"

"I have some bad news for you, sir. Your wife passed away an hour ago. She responded well initially to the operation but had a relapse on the ward and passed away. I am very sorry, sir."

"No, no, this can't be happening to me."

"Is there anyone with you, sir?"

"No."

"Would you like me to send a liaison officer round to see you, sir?"

"No, no, thank you."

Paul put the phone down. There was little else to be said.

"What time is it?" Paul asked himself out loud.

He went downstairs, emptied the remains of the whisky bottle into the tumbler. He went into the lounge, turning on the TV. A spaghetti western was on. What was he going to do now?

7

"Mr Kim?"

"Yes, who is this?"

"It's Joseph, sir, at Moore's Jewellers."

"Oh, hello Joseph, what can I do for you today?"

"It's the other way around, Mr Kim. Paul Moore has just phoned me to say that he will not be in for at least another week, as his wife has died."

"Oh, dear me. He is having a terrible time. Thank you for letting me know… Perkins, are we ready for the search of the accountants at Old Trafford?"

"Yes, sir. Just waiting for you."

"That was Joseph at Moore's Jewellers, to tell me that Mrs Moore, who was taken to Wythenshawe Hospital after her car crash, has died."

"That will cause Paul Moore even more headaches."

"Yes, so let's get on with this search."

A procession of police cars, Kim's Jaguar, and three

people carriers full of police officers left the police station. They were all prepared for a raid and search of Broadway Accountants and Aktaion Finance offices and their other companies. The building was a four-storey brick Victorian building on a terrace with access walkways every third property for rear access. A chip shop occupied the ground floor. An ideal location on match days being so close to Old Trafford and Manchester United's ground. Shut now, possibly only opened in the evenings and match days.

Two of the cars plus Jon Kim's pulled into the wide pavement forecourt used for parking, while the police vans parked on the road, despite double yellow lines. Three officers went around the back of the premises while Kim and Perkins pressed the bell.

Eventually, they were permitted access. A young lady greeted Kim and Perkins at the top of a steep set of stairs. The aroma in the hallway was that of a fish and chip shop. Even though it was days since the shop would have been open, the smell lingered.

Kim showed his warrant card, as did Perkins, to the young lady. Also, they gave her a copy of the warrant that permitted them to carry out a detailed search of the premises.

"None of the partners are here, sir; I don't think I can let you in without their agreement."

"Well, you can; this is a legal document giving us the right to carry out a detailed search of the premises."

"Can I ring one of the partners, sirs?"

She phoned a partner. He requested to be put through to Kim.

"Mr Cracknell wants to speak to you, sir."

She handed the telephone to Jon Kim.

"Who am I talking to?" demanded Cracknell.

"I am DCI Jon Kim of Greater Manchester Police. We have a warrant to search your premises and the offices of one of your clients, Aktaion Limited, who we understand occupy the floor above you?"

"That is correct, Mr Kim. Why didn't you provide prior warning of this search?"

"Prior warning is not what we do. It would defeat the object. We are commencing the search now, sir. I will be pleased to discuss this matter with you if you are returning to your office?"

"Yes, I will, inconvenient as it is." Cracknell slammed the phone down.

"Okay, guys, crack on," instructed Kim.

The officers spread out around the first floor and the second floor. They looked for any information or files relating to Graham Phillips, Paul Moore, the golf club, Aktaion Finance, and Aktaion Holdings.

While the search progressed, Perkins and Kim went to the top floor where the offices of Aktaion were situated. The door was locked, a bell push with a camera.

"Can I help you?" said the bell push.

"We are police officers," holding their warrant cards to the camera, "please allow us access."

"What do you want?"

"If you let us in, I will tell you what we are doing here."

"I have strict instructions not to allow anyone in without prior notice."

During this conversation between Kim and an unknown lady behind the door, Perkins had found the officer who had the 'enforcer' – a heavy metal tube with handles used for breaking down doors. The officer arrived. Kim told the person not to stand behind the door. "Keep clear."

The officer with the enforcer commenced

hammering the door, expecting it to be challenging to open. As it happened, the first blow at the door opened it easily. A middle-aged lady met them with a distinctive seventies-style tight perm to her auburn hair; spectacles that were like bottle bottoms. A beige jumper and tweed skirt completed the picture. She could have been standing on the side of a Scottish loch.

"What on earth do you think you are doing breaking in here?" she exploded.

"Madam, I am DCI Kim of GMP. Here is a copy of our warrant to search these premises. We gave you every opportunity to provide us with access. As you wouldn't open the door, we had to use force and enter. Please do not obstruct my officers any further, or you will find yourself arrested."

"Huh," she puffed. "I am about to phone my boss Graham Phillips; he will put a stop to this nonsense."

"As you wish, madam. I know Mr Phillips."

Four uniformed police officers entered the offices of Aktaion and commenced searching. After a few moments, one officer said the filing cabinet was locked. Kim requested the key.

"Madam, can you please let us have the key for this cabinet?"

"No, not without getting clearance from Mr Phillips."

"I will give you one more chance. What is your name?"

"Margaret Frances."

"Well, Margaret, I will give you one more chance to open the cabinet. If not, you will be arrested."

Without further comment, she opened her desk drawer, took out many keys, and opened the filing cabinet.

In Broadway Accountants' offices, the partner Jim Cracknell had arrived and was stamping around the office trying to prevent police officers from opening drawers and filing cabinets.

Jon Kim arrived and asked Mr Cracknell to co-operate, or he would be arrested. He was less than amused by the police actions but had little choice but to agree that they had the authority to do what they were doing.

Jon returned to the floor above and Aktaion's office. As he walked into the general office, he inadvertently knocked over a stick stand that held half a dozen sticks of one sort or another. The sticks rattled to the wooden floor, making a racket as they did so.

"Sorry, I didn't spot the stand as I was coming in. Quite a collection of interesting sticks." Jon began picking the various sticks up one by one. As he was doing so, he inspected the top of each stick. Some were quite ornamental; one had a silver knob, while another was considerably heavier than the other sticks.

"Quite an interesting lot of sticks?"

"Yes, they all belong to Mr Phillips. He sometimes takes one home and brings another from his collection at home. I use a stick every day," advised Margaret.

"And why is that?"

"Well, I live quite close to here, and I find a stick a great help with my walking. It would also provide me with some protection if I were attacked."

Looking at Margaret, Jon could not help seeing a Stag painting on the wall for the first time. It could only be a copy of Sir Edwin Landseer's famous painting, Monarch of the Glen.

"That is a wonderful painting. Contemporary with the building, Landseer was a wonderful artist. This must be his most famous work."

"Yes, it is. The reason the company is called Aktaion, is because of this picture."

"Oh, what do you mean?"

"Well, I imagine as a Chinese man, you will not be familiar with Greek mythology?"

"Correct, so why is this stag the influence for the name of the company?"

"The company's name was one that Peter Moore decided on when he joined. He changed the name of the company. He is, sorry was, a bit strong-headed in certain ways, and this was, I suppose, his way to put his mark on the company."

"I see, so tell me the background to the name, please?"

"Well Inspector, in Greek mythology, Aktaion was an accomplished hunter. He would hunt stags with dogs. One day, in mythology, he was out hunting and came upon a lake hidden deep in the forest. Artemis, otherwise known as Diana, goddess of hunting and chastity, was bathing in a pool naked. Once Aktaion spied her bathing, he was transfixed. Artemis, furious that he had spied on her, threw a handful of water over Aktaion in a rage. It transformed Aktaion into a stag. Only his mind remained human. He tried to run away, but his twenty-strong pack of hunting dogs fell upon him and tore him to pieces. As the company is involved with numerous business sectors hunting out the best deals for people, it was felt as Aktaion was such a skilful hunter his name would be appropriate for the company."

"What about the killing of Aktaion? Doesn't that concern the owners? Surely the way he met his end, being hunted, would signify that could be the final act for a member of the company?"

"I think you see things that don't exist, Inspector. The directors have just borrowed the name."

"How did you get on with Peter Moore?"

"We got on," replied Margaret.

"From that answer, I rather gather your feelings towards Mr Moore were not as amicable as they might be?"

"That's a fair summation, Inspector."

"Did you see Peter Moore on Friday, Margaret?"

Her response was hesitant as she tried to recall the events of that day.

"No, I don't think I did."

"What was it that upset you about Peter Moore?"

"Well, I worked for Graham Phillips in the surveying business for twelve years. When he set up

Phillips Financial Services, he arranged for me to be transferred without loss of benefits. My transfer was part of the sale agreement."

"So, is it fair to say you felt, or in fact were, the guardian of Mr Phillips' interests on a day-to-day basis?"

"Yes, that's a good way to put it."

"So, what upsets you about Peter Moore other than the change of name?"

"Well, he is dead now, so it doesn't matter."

"It matters to me, Margaret. What was he doing that upset you?"

"He took far too much money from the business. More than Mr Phillips. This was on the basis that he ran the firm and brought in new business."

"Was that true?"

"No, not really, it was Mr Phillips' good name in the business that brought us new customers. Admittedly Moore dealt with their requirements, but he was not the instigator of the work."

"Okay, Margaret, is there anything else you would like to tell me?"

"Just that I did go to the Imperial Hotel on Friday. Peter Moore phoned me to say he had mistakenly picked up Graham Phillips' jacket at the golf club. Could I collect it and bring it to the office for Graham to collect. Peter said he would not be in the office this week."

"So, did you see him and collect the jacket?"

"No, he was not in, and the receptionist would not give me access to Peter's room while he was absent."

"Okay, Margaret, what time would that be?"

"Well, I left just after five; I went home, collected my car and drove to the hotel. I know it well as we have held seminars there. I used the back entrance from the residents' car park. Peter told me the room number, 608, from memory. I knocked on the door, but there was no reply."

"What did you do then?"

"I tried to get the 'jobsworth' chap at the front desk to ask housekeeping to open the room for me."

"Did they do that?"

"No, they didn't, so I left."

"What time would that be?"

"About five forty-five, I recall as the news was just starting on the radio when I drove into my drive."

"Thanks, I think we will be out of your hair quite

soon," said Kim.

"How are things going, boys?" turning to speak to a police officer engaged in the search.

"I have some files here, sir, and a computer that we need to take away."

"Okay, please make an inventory of the items removed and give a copy to Margaret."

*

Back at Broadway Accountants' offices, Jon Kim met with Jim Cracknell, who was kicking off about the disruption caused to his business.

"Sir, I am DCI Kim; we have a warrant to carry out our search. It concerns the murder of Peter Moore, who I am sure you know. We have to seek out every possible bit of evidence to try and identify the murderer."

Cracknell was still not satisfied and spent the next twenty minutes on the phone to his solicitor.

After two hours, the police were finishing their search on both premises. They removed two computers and roughly twenty files.

"Mr Cracknell, I have the authority to remove this equipment and files. You will receive them back once we have completed our investigation. If you want to complain, there is an area on the GMP website to enable you to do that. The data and files we have taken all relate to your clients who trade under the Aktaion banner."

Kim and Perkins left the premises. The police officers were loading the items they had removed from the premises into a van then to GMP Headquarters.

"Quite a haul, Perkins, I will be interested to learn what you find when you have a good look at all the stuff." Perkins was not amused by the task he had just been set.

8

Paul Moore was in a terrible state. He had no one to turn to. His son's death, his wife and his brother in one week were more than anyone should be asked to cope with.

He dressed in casual outdoor clothes in anticipation of a walk. He planned a walk from Pownall Park down to 'The Carrs', a park area bisected by the River Bollin. He would walk to the Parish Church, then possibly call in at the Church Inn, then home.

It was half past ten when he left his front door. He had left his mobile phone behind on purpose. He could stand no more of the constant calls from unexpected people.

The weather was slightly overcast, yet the sun came out in patches. When it did appear, the temperature rose; it even became pleasant.

His mind was racing. There were going to be so many difficult things to arrange. Three funerals, wills, solicitors, his future. What was he going to do? He was so transfixed with his thoughts he failed to hear the call of 'Paul' from the other side of the road. Before he knew it, he was confronted by a lady wearing a bright blue anorak. Her blonde hair was just visible under her woollen hat. Paul looked quizzically at this person; he was sure he knew but could not recall her name.

"Paul, it's me, Judy."

"Judy, how are you?"

"More to the point, how are you? What a terrible time you are having, so I hear."

A tear began to trickle down Paul's face. Judy realised he was very distraught.

"Are you going for a walk?" she asked.

"Yes, a quiet long one so I can think and plan. I am going via the 'Carrs'; I want to call in at the church, then back home." Paul hoped she would assume the Parish Church, not the pub.

"Would you like me to come with you, Paul?"

"How do I say no, without being offensive, Judy?"

"You will never be offensive in my eyes, Paul. Just let me know if you would like some company, I will pop over. How are you doing for food?"

"Fine, no problem. Hope to see you soon, Judy."

She realised he needed space, so she gave him a peck on the cheek and let him go his way. Judy went in the opposite direction.

Paul was delighted she had moved on; he wanted some space and a time to think.

*

"Perkins, where does Peter Moore live?"

"I can tell you, sir; his address is in the personnel file from Aktaion."

"Good, we should go and have a look at the place. Have we a set of keys that we might have recovered?"

"No sir, there were no keys in Graham Phillips' jacket. We better ask a team to come with us to gain access."

That was organised, and the two police officers motored to a block of modern apartments adjoining the Salford Media City complex. The tall buildings had been constructed to create a media village. The cluster of tall buildings had been oriented in such a way as to provide a feeling of space.

Parking in the visitors' car park with the police van next to them, the four officers found their way to the lifts that would take them to the twelfth floor.

"It's apartment, 1204, sir."

"That sounds like it is at the top or nearly at the top." The other two officers joined them in the lift, one carrying an enforcer.

The lift deposited the four policemen on a landing with signs indicating the way to go. Right or left. The right was for odd numbers, and the left for even numbers. The flat 1204 was then going to be south facing. Jon Kim invited the police constable with the enforcer to break in. He just touched the door, and it swung open.

Kim went in with Perkins, shouting out that it was the police. As they arrived in the lounge area, Margaret Frances called out – "I will be with you in a moment."

"What are you doing here, Margaret?"

"I thought I would come and tidy up and make the place look reasonable, as the flat will surely be put up for sale."

"Are you a beneficiary of Peter's will or an executor?"

"No, I am not. I am here simply to do the decent thing."

"Have you taken anything from the flat, or are you about to remove anything?"

"No, apart from food that is near its sell-by date and kitchen waste which will go down the refuse chute."

"Have you ever been here before?"

"Yes, several times."

"Do you have a key to the apartment and a key for the main doorway?"

"Yes, I do, Inspector."

"Why is that?"

"Well, Peter used to ask me to buy food for him and put it in the fridge. I needed keys to manage that."

"When we spoke last about Peter Moore, you led me to believe you were not very friendly towards him. Now you tell me you did his shopping for him, and here you are tidying his flat. Your relationship was somewhat closer than you would have me believe. Isn't that so?"

"I don't know where you got that impression; I was not always cordial towards Peter, that is true. My loyalty is indeed to Graham Phillips, but that doesn't mean I can't be civil to another member of staff."

"Where have you been cleaning and tidying?"

"Just in here and the bathroom and kitchen."

"Where is the waste you are throwing away?"

"I have it all in a plastic bag; it's over there," she said, pointing to a plastic waste bag by the door."

"To save you the trouble, we will take that away for you."

"Thank you, Inspector, is there anything else you need to see?"

"Why do you suppose we found no keys on his body that give access to this flat?"

"I really couldn't say, Inspector. Have you checked his car?"

"Yes, we will when we locate it. I will just have a good look around. If you let me have the keys, we will lock up when we are finished. I cannot imagine you have any further matters to deal with in here, which requires you to hold the keys?"

"Very well, here they are. I will go now." Margaret left the flat, handing the keys to Jon Kim; she threw the keys into Jon's hand. Margaret was furious. Her face was flushed. She left, slamming the door behind her.

"Perkins, we need to find something with the chance that her fingerprints will be on the surface. Probably best to get SOCO in here as soon as they can. Let's lock up and go. Bring the rubbish bag with you; we can take it back to the station."

All four police officers left the flat and locked it.

"Has anyone got the 'Police Incident no entry' stickers on them?"

Everyone confirmed that they did not have the stickers.

"Make a note, Perkins, get SOCO to secure the premises and stick the 'no entry' label on the door."

*

Back at GMP HQ, Jon started to consider all the evidence they had so far collected. He considered all the following: -

'The jacket' belonging to Graham Phillips, how did it get to the bedroom where Peter Moore was found? It was last seen in the golf club. Did Peter Moore take it to the room as Margaret had said? Was it Peter Moore himself or someone else? That other person could be Graham Phillips, Paul Moore, Margaret Frances although unlikely, who had admitted going to the hotel, and Major Rupert Ives who had left the golf club early on Friday. Who would have the most to benefit from Peter Moore's death?

At the time of the murder, several people had access to Peter Moore's room on Friday, sometime between three in the afternoon and six. Graham Phillips, Paul Moore, Margaret Frances, Major Rupert Ives, potentially Jim Cracknell, and finally, with no good reason to do this deed, Joseph White. Looking at the suspects one by one, would Graham Phillips have murdered Peter? Why would he do that? He had chosen him to run his business. Paul Moore, perhaps, but why? He was at the golf club most of the day. The Imperial Hotel would be out of his way. According to the PR files, Margaret Frances may have a grudge that Peter was brought in to run Phillips' business; she was side-lined, and Peter was being paid about three times the amount she received. She said she had visited the Imperial but Peter was not there. Was that true, or was he there, and she murdered him? He could not have answered reception if he was already dead. She would have needed to kill Peter Moore before asking reception to call his room. Not very likely.

Rupert Ives, possibly the only one with the experience to commit murder, but what would he gain from that? Could he expect to inherit some of the shareholdings Peter Moore had, which would give him more income and a more significant say in the running of Aktaion?

The murder weapon. A blade, a long thin blade. At least half a metre long. What weapon would be that long? A sword, a bayonet, or a long knife. Margaret could have done that; she did admit she used a stick regularly. She also accessed the hotel from the rear. Indeed, they had CCTV covering the back. If she was holding a stick on her way in, they needed to arrest her as soon as they could.

"Perkins, can you arrange a copy of the CCTV covering the rear entrance for the afternoon of the murder?" demanded Kim.

'Motive' – who had a motive for killing Peter Moore? Anyone with a grudge or who believed he was siphoning money from his firm illegally. So that might be Graham Phillips, Margaret Frances, Major Rupert Ives, less likely Paul Moore, and Joseph White.

Jon couldn't think of another motive other than money. It was the most potent reason for dispatching someone. Who would benefit from Peter Moore's death? It was reasonable to assume that Graham Phillips would be one, but he put Moore in place, so presumably, Phillips himself would not need to work as hard as he had previously. Then there was Rupert

Ives; with fewer directors, the more money there would be to go round. Kim couldn't work out why Margaret Frances would benefit from his death.

Could Paul Moore see a benefit from Peter's death? He was the one person who was hard up. Who would be acting in respect of Peter Moore's estate? Was there any value there? Who would be the primary beneficiaries?

Jon started to re-read the SOCO report, and the pathologist's report. There was no doubt that a drug had been administered. The pathologist was waiting to find out what drug had been used.

"Hi, this is DCI Jon Kim. Do you have the report back regarding the drug you suspected had been used on Peter Moore?"

"Yes, sir, we emailed you a report an hour ago."

"Okay, thanks, I have been busy with something else. I should have checked my inbox. Thanks."

Jon checked his inbox; there was the email he expected, it stated: -

'There were traces of dissolved Flunitrazepam (Rohypnol) in one of the glasses. Vodka and Coke drinks would have masked the dissolved Rohypnol, which has a blue colour when dissolved in a colourless liquid. There were no fingerprints on the glass without traces of the drug.'

"Damn," Jon stated out loud to no one. All we need is to find the source of the drug, which would undoubtedly ensure we would identify the culprit. How would Margaret get hold of Rohypnol?

"Any traces of anything of interest in the waste bag, Perkins?"

"No, sir, I am sorry, there is nothing of interest. Possibly two halves of a green pill casing that's all, but no contents."

"That needs to go to forensics. It is possibly a Rohypnol case. We need to find the source of supply of the Rohypnol; if we can do that, I guess we can nail our culprit."

9

Paul Moore was beginning to realise what had happened to him and his family. He still woke expecting to find Di next to him, never to happen again. He was sitting in the lounge, musing on the days ahead with two or three funerals, if Peter's body would be released to him for cremation.

The phone rang.

"Not another nosy parker."

After a few rings, Paul decided to answer it, and it could be significant.

"Hello, Mr Moore?" said a Chinese voice.

"Yes, that's me; who are you?"

"I am Bao's mother. I am in Shanghai, China."

"I am so sorry about Bao; I hope he is making good progress?"

"Yes, we have him here in China now. He was flown to us over the weekend. I just wanted to say how sorry we are that you lost your son in the accident. Bao and Richard were good friends."

"Yes, I know. I am so glad he is with you now."

"Well, I just wanted to thank you and your wife for your kind gesture in inviting Bao for the exeat weekend."

Paul lost control for a moment with a cry, which was transmitted to China.

"Mr Moore, I am sorry, I didn't mean to upset you."

"It's just that you mentioned my wife as well as Richard. They are both dead."

"Oh, I had no idea. I am so sorry. Thank you again. I hope things work out for you. Bye."

The phone went dead. Paul was now in a state of depression and anxiety. What would he do?

Paul had just put the phone down, and it rang again.

"Can I speak with Paul Moore, please?"

"Who wants to speak to him?" Paul answered in a testy voice.

"I do. Toby Kerslake, Peter Moore's solicitor. Are you Paul Moore?"

"Yes, I am."

"I assume, sir, you are aware your twin brother was murdered last Friday?"

"Yes, the worst day of my life."

"How is that, sir?"

"Well, not only was my twin brother killed, but my wife and only child Richard were killed in a crash in the airport tunnels under the runway at Manchester Airport, Saturday lunchtime."

"Mr Moore, I am so terribly sorry, I had no idea. I saw the crash report on TV on Saturday night. You have my sincere condolences."

"Thank you, Mr Kerslake. What can I help you with?"

"Well, sir, as far as I can tell, and in accordance with the last will and testament of your brother, you are the sole heir to his estate. He was never married and had no descendants that I know of. Do you know of any that might still be alive?"

"No, I don't, so what does that mean?"

"Well, sir, I think the estate of your brother is quite substantial."

"Oh, please explain." Paul was now feeling a little less morbid.

"It means, sir, that all the assets and the benefit of life assurance policies come to you. Like most things, there is a process to undertake, but we can do this for you with your assistance."

"Okay, may I call you Toby? Please call me Paul. What do I do now?"

"Best thing Paul is for us to meet. I understand you live in Wilmslow. I live in Bramhall, so it is easy for me to call and see you. Would tomorrow at say ten in the morning be acceptable?"

"Yes, that would be fine."

Paul put the phone down, feeling somewhat excited at the prospect of some money from his brother's estate. "I can't believe it will be straightforward."

Feeling elated and sad all at once, coupled with a newfound hunger, Paul made a snack lunch. He was just loading the dishwasher when the phone rang again.

"Worth answering," he muttered to himself.

"Paul Moore, this is DCI Jon Kim GMP. I want to come and see you about your brother's murder."

"Okay, no problem. When do you want to come?"

"Four o'clock this afternoon."

"Okay, see you then."

Paul could not imagine what they needed to speak about now. "All will be revealed," he muttered to himself.

Jon Kim, accompanied by Perkins, arrived at ten to four. All three men retired to the lounge.

"How are you coping, Mr Moore?"

"Well, I have had better weeks. You probably know that both my wife and son were killed in the crash under the airport tunnel. My wife had to have a second operation; she died a short while after that when she returned to the ward."

"My goodness, you have had a real pasting. My condolences. My reason for coming is to enquire if either you, your wife or indeed your brother needed sleeping pills?"

"Not as far as I am aware. My wife used the second bathroom. I have not even thought to look at her medicine cabinet. We can do that now if you wish."

The three men went upstairs, and Paul navigated the way to Di's bathroom. The medicine cabinet with three mirrored doors at the front, mounted on the wall over the washbasin, was at first glance filled with cosmetics.

"Help yourselves, gentlemen."

"Is there another cabinet anywhere else in the house?" enquired Kim.

"Yes, there is one in 'my' bathroom; I will show you."

Kim went with Paul to a similar cabinet, this time filled with shaving equipment and aftershave. There were a few medicines, mainly over-the-counter stuff.

"Thanks, Mr Moore."

Kim called out to Perkins, "Have you spotted anything?"

"Your assistance would be appreciated," responded Perkins. "There are several prescription drugs all made out to Mrs Moore. I don't know what they are."

"Well, let's take them all and get our guys to tell us what we have here."

"Do you have any objection to us removing these drugs, sir? We need to get them tested and checked for what they might be."

"No, Inspector, help yourself. If you would like a plastic bag, I have some in the kitchen."

Paul took a Tesco bag from the kitchen drawer and handed it to Perkins. Kim and Moore went back into the lounge.

"Can you tell me please, Mr Moore, what you were doing on Friday, and also what your wife was doing on Friday?"

"I can tell you what I was doing on Friday; I was at the golf match in Knutsford. I went to my work premises in Dale Street for a couple of hours in the morning, then I went to Knutsford for the golf match arriving at about noon."

"Okay, so what was your wife doing?"

"I don't know, she lived a separate life in the main, to me. She would most likely be shopping, then lunch in Wilmslow with some of her girlfriends. That you would think would last an hour, but no, the girls' lunches went on for three hours or more."

"Do you know any of her friends who might have been with her?"

"Well, one, in particular, her name is Judy, she lives about six houses down from here."

"Okay, we will need to speak to her. Perkins, can you take down her address?"

"I have a swab here, Mr Moore; it's a DNA test. Can you please help us eliminate you by allowing me to take a sample of saliva on this cotton bud and sealing it into the tube? Your DNA will not be held longer than is necessary until our enquiries are complete."

That done, Kim and Perkins left.

Knocking on the door, Judy came to the door dressed in her tracksuit, as though she was about to go for a run. Once Kim had concluded the introductions, she invited them in.

There was only one topic of conversation in the large kitchen as far as the police were concerned. Judy wanted to know all about the investigation.

"On Friday last, I gather you had lunch with Diana and others? Where did you take lunch?" requested Kim.

"That's easy; we mostly met on a Friday for lunch. We usually met at a hotel just outside Wilmslow, The Bollin, which is the river's name that flows through its grounds. There were five of us, including Diana and me. Isn't her name wonderful? Greek mythology says Diana was also called Artemis, the goddess of her favourite pursuit of hunting. She was also the fierce queen of celibacy chastity and virginity."

"Why did you choose this hotel for lunch?"

"Easy car parking. We all have a big four-by-four cars. Diana's is the newest and possibly the most expensive."

"Was that important?"

"Oh, yes, you have to show off. Cheshire Housewives, you know."

"No, I don't know. How long were you at lunch? When did you all arrive at The Bollin?"

"We normally expected to arrive at noon, then we would stay until about three."

"Did Diana stay to the end?"

"No, in fact, a couple of people left about two-thirty."

"Do you know where she was going?"

"No, we didn't ask questions like that, especially when we knew her husband was away for the day playing golf."

"Is there something I am missing in what you have just said?"

"Well, you are a man of the world. We all suspected that most of the girls had a boyfriend on the go somewhere."

"Do you have one, Judy?"

"Why not? But I am not going to tell you who it is."

"Was it her 'boyfriend' that Diana was going to meet?"

"I have no idea, Inspector. I am sure if she were, she wouldn't tell me I am a terrible gossip."

"Okay, thank you, Judy, you have been most helpful."

10

Back at GMP headquarters, Kim had a message on his phone to ring a Sergeant Evans in Traffic.

"Sergeant, I am Jon Kim; you left a message for me to ring you."

"Yes, sir, I am the officer dealing with the crash in which Mrs Diana Moore was injured, her son died, and his friend broke both legs."

"Yes, okay, I can see the overlap."

"Well, sir, we have some effects belonging to Mrs Moore taken from her car. We would, in normal cases, return the items to her husband, but given the enquiry you have and the connection the Moores, I thought you might like these effects, and a copy of the post-mortem report which I am sure you will find interesting. Mrs Moore was about eight weeks pregnant."

"Wow, was she? That is interesting. Who did the PM?"

"The pathologist at the MRI in their mortuary. Dr Singh, I believe."

"Do you know if they still have the body?" enquired Kim.

"Possibly, sir, I can give you the number. It will be in order for you to call and enquire."

Thanking the sergeant, Kim rang Dr Singh.

"Yes, Inspector, we were about to release the body to the undertakers."

"Can you provide me with one other piece of information? I need to know the DNA of the foetus; would that be possible?"

"Yes, sir, it would, but there is no need for me to do anything, I have already done that. I suspected someone might ask. I will forward the DNA report."

"Thank you. One more point on DNA, I am dealing with the murder of a twin. I would say they were identical as I was sure I knew the dead man, but it was his twin who had been murdered. Is there a difference between the DNA of twins?"

"Good question, Inspector. For the most part, with identical twins, their DNA will match."

"So, if that is the case, how could you tell between

one twin and another who was responsible for the foetus? In the case of Mrs Diana Moore, her husband is a twin, his brother was murdered."

"No, it would not, in that case, be possible to determine which brother was the father of the unborn child."

"Ah, well, thank you anyway."

Within the hour, Kim had received items from the Range Rover and the DNA report from the MRI.

"Perkins, what did you do with the waste from Peter Moore's flat?"

"I put it out for disposal, sir, as you requested."

"Okay, see if it is still there and ask a courier to come from pathology; I have several items that need investigating."

Kim now phoned the pathology department of GMP.

"Hi, DCI Kim here. Do you still hold the body of Peter Moore? The murder victim from the Imperial Hotel?"

"Yes, sir."

"Have you made DNA tests?"

"Yes, sir, it is routine now."

"Okay, can I send you a DNA swab to see what it turns up?"

"Yes, sir, no problem."

Kim now returned to see Margaret Frances at the offices of Aktaion, at Old Trafford.

"Margaret, it's Jon Kim from the police. Can I come in, please?"

"Yes, Mr Kim." The door buzzer sounded, and he obtained access to the offices.

"I am very interested in the sticks, the ones I knocked over when I was here last."

"Oh, and why would they be of interest?"

"Just part of my enquiries. How many sticks are in the stand?"

"That's a straightforward question. Six, there are always six unless I have taken one for my walk."

"Okay, so can I have another look at them?"

"Of course."

Jon went to the stick holder; he counted five. Pulling one of the sticks out, he made a mental note about them. One was a Malacca cane, the next a stick with a silver knob on the top, the next a narwhal tusk, used as a stick, the next a traditional walking stick with a rubber end, the final one was a thicker stick with a handle in bone, and a ferrule that looked like brass. It was a very heavy stick.

"There are only five sticks here, Margaret."

"That's odd; someone has taken one out, they usually tell me."

"Who would that 'other person' be?"

"Possibly Peter Moore. He was in the habit of borrowing a stick quite often, usually on a Friday. I assumed he would be walking over the weekend. He always returned it on Monday."

"I can work out four of the sticks, but there is one here that is heavier than the other sticks, is there a reason for that?"

"Yes, Mr Kim, we have two like that."

"So, what is so special about them?"

"Well, let me show you." Margaret walked over to the stick stand picking out the stick in question. "These sticks are quite rare and valuable. It is called a sword-stick, and it is from the early Victorian period. They are worth four to five hundred pounds."

"So, what does it do, Margaret?"

"Let me show you," she said, twisting the ferrule at

the top just below the handle and then pulled out the sword blade.

"That is truly amazing. I have never seen anything like that before. So, what were they used for?"

"In the late eighteenth century and throughout the nineteenth century, when police were not so readily available in the event of an attack on a person, a gentleman would have a sword-stick and pull out the blade to protect himself from attack. Or indeed attack the attacker. These are deadly weapons."

"Yes, I can see that, Margaret. So, there should be another one of these in the stick bin?"

"Yes, it should be in here. I guess Peter Moore has, or should I say did borrow it."

"Thanks, Margaret. That was very useful."

Returning to GMP, Jon was full of excitement as he now knew what the murder weapon looked like.

"DCI Kim, there is a courier at the front desk with several items for you."

"Send him up, please."

A few moments later, a courier staggered into the detective's office with two paper bags full of items.

Jon couldn't wait to open the packages. He put on

some latex gloves before opening the first bag. It was long and could be the missing walking stick. He was correct; it was a sword stick. "This needs to go to forensics," he said to himself.

The next bag held Diana's handbag. Jon couldn't wait to have a rummage. Out came two sets of keys, a handkerchief, some perfume, two tablets in a foil strip, her mobile phone, a wallet with cash and credit cards, and a pregnancy testing kit. Also, from traffic were items usually found in a car, road atlas, dusters, torch, etc. *Nothing to excite me here.*

*

Paul Moore was waiting for Toby Kerslake, who he had invited to call at four o'clock. It was nearly that now. Paul equipped himself with a paper and pen.

He was about to settle down to wait, and the front doorbell rang. It was Toby.

Introductions over, they agreed that first names were appropriate.

"So, you have had a terrible time, Paul. You have my commiserations."

"Thank you, Toby. I don't have a personal solicitor. Are you able to act for me?"

"Yes, we can act for you. The Law Society sees beneficiaries as clients of the executor's lawyers. Very often, the deceased lawyer is an executor as well."

"I am glad about that as there are some issues concerning my wife and son I have to deal with, and I am not sure what to do."

"Okay, let's start with your brother's estate. I was involved in drawing up his will. I know of no other, so we can for these purposes assume that this document is his last will and testament."

"Okay, I am sure you are right."

"There are various bequests to you, your son and your wife. Unusually the largest amount goes to your wife – a smaller sum to your son, the balance of the estate to you. The main bequests are from a life insurance policy. For this conversation, and for simplicity, I will treat all the bequests as one. They will all come to you, as there is no other beneficiary and your wife and son are both dead, the total sum will come to you."

"I understand; why would Peter leave more money to Diana, as opposed to me?"

"I am sorry, I was not acquainted with the reasons behind the bequests. The assets on your brother's estate are a life assurance policy with Legal and General, some ISAs, with the same company, there is some money in the bank. Also, there is a flat in Media City and his BMW car. Some smaller items and contents have value, but I have ignored them for the moment. He has a shareholding in Aktaion Holdings. His shareholding, according to Companies House, is thirty per cent of the equity. There may be a shareholders' agreement; if so, could you see if you can obtain a copy of it? There may be timescales for the existing directors to make a bid. We also need a copy of last year's accounts or this year if available."

"Yes, I am sure I can do that, Toby."

"Okay, well, leaving the car, the company, and contents out of the picture, the estate values are as follows: the life insurance is worth one million, the ISAs are worth one hundred and twenty thousand pounds. The apartment's net value, which will have to be professionally valued, is, I think, about two hundred and fifty thousand pounds. Then there is the car, say ten thousand. So, in cash terms, the estate's total value, excluding the value of his shares in Aktaion, is worth about one million, three hundred and eighty thousand pounds. Regrettably, there is inheritance tax to pay.

"The calculation of IHT is quite complex, and we

shall require an accountant and some valuations, including the value of Peter's share in Aktaion.

"There is a tax-free sum for the beneficiary of three hundred and twenty-five thousand pounds. The net amount then is approximately one million and fifty-five thousand pounds. The tax on that at the current rate of forty per cent is four hundred and twenty-two thousand pounds.

"Adding back the tax-free sum to the after-tax sum, the net amount you will get is about nine hundred and fifty-eight thousand pounds. So, despite the tax, it is still a significant sum. I realise it can't bring people back, but it would take a long time to save that sort of money."

"I hadn't realised that that amount of tax would be payable. It is an enormous sum. What I need help with is the procedure for funerals and cremation. Do I just contact an undertaker?"

"Yes, he will be able to speak with the police and obtain a coroner's burial certificate. That's what it is called, but it covers cremations as well. Have you thought about what you might do next?"

"No, Toby, I am shell shocked. I have no idea. I need some time. I may go away for a couple of weeks to get my head back in place once the funerals are over."

"That sounds very sensible. Now don't forget to let me have details of the shareholding and a copy of the shareholder's agreement if there is one."

"No, I won't. Thank you for all your help. Is there anything you want me to do now?"

"Other than the items I have already mentioned, no. I will get the death certificate from the coroner's office and make the claims."

"Thanks, Toby, keep in touch."

Despite his distress, Paul was quietly delighted that the sum of approaching a million was soon to land on his lap. What to do next and where to go was the question.

11

"Judy, this is Jon Kim. Could I come and speak with you today, please? What time would suit you?"

"Oh, Mr Kim, I will be leaving home for lunch at eleven-thirty. If you could come over by ten this morning, that would be great."

"Yes, I can do that; I will leave Manchester now."

Jon collected his pad, mobile phone, as he was leaving the office at twenty past nine. It was a bit of a stretch to get to Wilmslow by ten. The M56 would help as he needed to put his foot down.

On his way to Wilmslow Jon, called Paul Moore – hands-free – telling him he wanted to speak to him at around eleven o'clock, which was agreed.

Jon arrived at Judy's house at five past ten.

"Good morning. Sorry to be a few minutes late, there was a great deal of traffic at the junction with the M56 where they are creating a new access for the large industrial estate where the new Amazon warehouse is being constructed."

"No worries, Jon, come in. Would you like a coffee?"

"Thank you, just black."

"So, what can I do for you, Jon?"

"Well, as a self-confessed gossip, I thought you must have had a conversation with Diana either before or at your lunch on Friday and before her car crash on Saturday?"

"You mean you want me to disclose secrets?"

"If indeed it is a secret. With your friend dead, it can hardly be a problem."

"I see what you mean. Yes, we did have a big heart-to-heart; you see, she was having an affair with her brother-in-law. Quite odd, it would be like shagging your husband, but it wasn't him!"

"I had gathered that was going on."

"Really? Well, Peter was quite astute. After the first time, he was concerned that Di would let the cat out of the bag, and that would be a problem; you see, we do tend to chat. So, they agreed Di would take half a pill's worth of Rohypnol. They could have sex, yet she would not recall what happened."

"A bit devious and very trusting on Diana's part."

"Well, you see, the thing is that Di would not have sex with Peter unless he wore a condom. That was established from the off. He played the game once when she was out of it on Rohypnol. The second time he realised that she would never know if he was wearing a condom or not. He preferred sex without. Later, Di felt she was sure she was pregnant; you see, her period didn't come. She got a test kit from Boots; she tested positive. She was not going to have an abortion, so what was she to do?"

"I see, so she would have to own up to Paul and have the child. That would bugger up her social life. I have reason to believe Richard was adopted, is that correct?"

"You are quite correct, Jon. Paul could not create children as after tests; it was discovered he was firing blanks. How did you find that out, Jon?"

"Using DNA, Richard could not be related to Paul and Diana. So, what did Diana decide to do?"

"Di and Peter had a row; he was insisting she should have an abortion. She was brought up as a Roman Catholic, and her belief forbade her from having an abortion. They agreed to meet one more time, and that time was the Friday before her crash, and instead of meeting in Peter's flat, they were going to meet at the Imperial Hotel, as Peter was going to the match on Saturday. Well, she told me she could kill Peter as he had abused her and made her forget what happened. I am sure she didn't kill him; it was just a figure of speech as you do."

"Okay, well, I don't suppose there was much else he could say or do?"

"No, but she thought she would do a Fifty Shades of Grey on Peter and switch drinks so he could be knocked out; she was going to make him suffer."

"Mm, she was wound up about this."

"Yes, she was going to make Peter suffer as she had decided in the end to have an abortion, but Paul didn't need to know anything about her decision. So, as she was going to have to suffer, and it wasn't her fault, she was going to make Peter suffer. A dose of Rohypnol for him would make her actions so much easier, not having to fight off a man."

"Diana told you all this?"

"Yes, it was so exciting, the whole group knew what was going to happen to Peter that afternoon. I just had to tell them all, once Di had left early for her assignation with Peter."

"As you recall this so vividly, can you tell me what she was wearing that day?"

"Well, we all dress up for lunch. Di had purchased a new burnt orange dress which came up to the neck in a little stand-up collar. The back was where the interest was. The back's whole length was a large and obvious zip, right down from the neck to her bum. She wore the dress without a bra, wearing the dress with the zip undone partway down her back. Talk about sexy, or what? It was fabulous."

"Well, Judy, I have discovered a great deal more than I anticipated. Thank you. I just wished you had told me all this at the beginning. Thanks for the coffee."

*

It was just past eleven when Jon drove a few hundred yards to the front of Paul Moore's house.

Paul saw him arrive and opened the front door.

"Thank you for seeing me, Paul. I need to ask a few questions."

"Okay, I guess there can't be too many more; you must know all about us by now."

"This question is personal, but I need to know. Was Richard adopted?"

"Yes, how on earth did you know that?"

"Well, DNA these days is so easy to do and has become standard practice. It was clear from the results Richard could not be biologically related to you and Diana."

The mention of her name brought a teardown of Paul's face.

"Mr Kim, this not something a man likes to admit, but my sperm is dead. I cannot create a child, so we decided after many tests to adopt. It transpired to be a great decision; Richard was a great kid."

"Okay, thanks. I am sorry to ask painful questions. On a lighter note, can you recall what Diana was wearing on the Friday before the crash? We have the clothes she was wearing on Saturday; I suspect she wore something different on Friday?"

"As far as I can recall, it was a pretty demure dress for Diana. It was orange with a high neck. There was a big zip at the back which was zipped all the way up."

"Would you know where that dress is now?"

"Well, it won't be in the laundry basket as that is for

clothes to be washed. We have another container on the landing for clothes to go to the dry cleaners. If it is in there, it was supposed to go to the cleaners on Monday. However, I would expect it to be in one of Di's wardrobes unless she spilt something down the dress at her lunch meeting with the girls."

"Do you mind if we have a look?" Jon had brought with him an evidence bag, just in case he came across the dress.

The dry-cleaning box was inspected, but it wasn't there. The two men searched the four fitted double wardrobes containing Di's clothes. They could not find the orange dress which would have stood out from the rest.

"I can't find it, Jon."

"Well, it might be possible if there was nothing else in the dry-cleaning box, she took it to the cleaners on Friday afternoon or Saturday morning?"

"Yes, that's true. Sorry I can't help you."

"Which cleaners did Diana use?"

"It's a small independent firm; they are on Chapel Lane. Their shop is close to the Co-op funeral shop."

"Okay, Paul, thanks for your help. I will be in touch

shortly once the coroner has done his bit and issued death certificates."

Jon drove to the dry cleaners, stopping opposite in a marked parking bay, making sure he wasn't going to have his door removed by traffic steaming down the road.

"Good morning. I am DCI Jon Kim of Greater Manchester Police. A Mrs Diana Moore was a regular customer – she recently brought a bright orange dress to you for cleaning. Do you still have it?"

After a long wait, the shop attendant came out from the back.

"Sorry, sir, we have been swamped; we haven't started it yet as it is a difficult colour and needs a lot of tomato soup removing. We can have it done by the morning."

"No, no, please don't do anything with it. I need to remove it from you and take it away for forensic investigation."

"Oh, so you don't want it cleaned now?" she said in a somewhat grumpy voice, believing she had lost a sale. She disappeared into the back, bringing the dress with her. Jon placed it in the evidence bag, then asked how much would it have cost to clean.

"Well, it was not an easy garment to clean with the long zip and all, probably ten pounds."

"I will give you the ten pounds, as you have lost a sale. Please can I have a receipt?" said Jon, passing a ten-pound note over the counter. She was delighted now.

Back at GMP HQ, Jon logged the dress in the evidence book and immediately sent it to forensics.

12

Two days later, Jon Kim had received the final forensic report. He was looking forward to seeing if his hunch was correct.

The report told Jon that the blood from Peter Moore caused the staining on the dress. The blood of Peter Moore, or Paul Moore, but as no injury had been indicated on Paul Moore, and he was still around, it was reasonable to assume the blood was Peter Moore's.

The report continued to deal with the sword stick. The blade's size and length would accord with the pathologist's account for the entry and exit wounds' length and size. The residue of blood around the hilt was the same as Peter Moore's blood.

The confusion as to what Jon could do next was concerning him. He had a murder victim, for sure a murderer, but they were both dead for the first time in his career. He decided to phone the Criminal Prosecution Service for advice.

"Can I speak to a senior lawyer, please? I am DCI

Kim GMP; it's about a murder."

"Mr Kim, what can I do for the GMP today?"

"Well, sir, I have a cast-iron case against a woman who has murdered her lover. She is pregnant by him and was furious at being put into that position. According to our pathologists, she drugged her lover with Rohypnol, a small dose, but enough to immobilise him. Having administered the drug in a mixture of vodka and Coke and allowed him to sit at a desk in his hotel bedroom, he started to write the word 'STAG' on a piece of paper.

"The word's significance is that his company's name is Aktaion, the Greek name of a hunter who was transformed into a stag. The mythological penalty for gazing on the naked body of Artemis, Aktaion's hunting dogs set on him and killed him.

"I believe that the unfinished word written at the moment of passing out from the drug is a guide to us regarding what was to befall him.

"His female lover stabbed the man through the desk chair and then through his heart with a sword stick. A thin blade that is hidden inside a walking stick. She was pregnant by this man; she was the murderer. We have forensic evidence, which is unquestionable.

She was Mrs Diana Moore, the sister-in-law of the murdered man. My problem, sir, is that the woman was killed in a car crash the following day, killing her adopted son. What is the position about laying charges?"

"Fascinating and comprehensive piece of detective work. However, I regret you have no one to lay charges on, so the case has to be dropped."

"Thank you, but what a complete waste of time."

"You may think that, Kim, but without your investigation, another detective might have incorrectly laid charges on an innocent man, which would be worse."

"What should I tell her husband?"

"Nothing, his grief is great; your finings will not help in his grieving. There is no point in advising him."

"What I didn't tell you, sir, is that the dead man is the twin brother of the woman's husband."

"I think, therefore, there is even less reason for advising the poor man. Please make a careful note on the file, including the final decision, making it clear you spoke with us. Then file it all away. There is one other issue which, as a police force, we may have to attend to."

"And what is that, sir?" enquired Kim.

"Well, if the dead twin has no heirs, and because of the affair with his sister-in-law he decided to leave some money to her, the insurers may not pay out the amount she was due to receive, as it could be argued she killed the man for the money."

"What do you advise, sir?"

"Well, Kim, if we are asked, we will have to tell the truth. However, we are not obliged to make our findings public. So, the name of the murderer would never be known. I say this as the poor husband, and twin brother will now get his brother's estate in total. If the insurers discover who had a financial interest in the estate of the dead man that she had murdered, they are most likely to refuse to pay that part of the endowment."

Jon Kim thanked the CPS lawyer. He called Perkins, the deputy CC, and a stenographer. The deputy CC agreed that a meeting could take place tomorrow in his office.

Jon Kim discovered the solicitor for Peter Moore, who he telephoned, to get Peter Moore's estate's bare bones. Jon was taken aback at the amounts involved.

The following day the meeting took place in the

deputy CC's office; the stenographer made a careful record for the file. Jon Kim explained the case in detail, ending with the advice from the CPS. At the end of the meeting, the deputy CC congratulated Kim and Perkins for a job well done.

As the deputy CC was leaving the room, Kim asked if he could have a quiet word. Kim explained the dilemma and how Paul Moore could lose the benefit of about half a million pounds if the insurers took the view Diana Moore had killed him for the cash.

"My problem is, sir: do we have to make public our findings?"

"Mm, we haven't had this conversation, Kim. Put the information you have given me in a sealed envelope at the end of the file. Close the case, and say no more. I have already forgotten what you said."

Later that day, Paul Moore phoned to tell Kim when the funerals would be, and that as a consequence of the murder and his wife and Richard dying, he was going to emigrate to Mallorca and run a small bar. Everything he owned in the UK would be sold. Kim wished him well.

"Mr Phillips, I have your jacket and contents. We have no further use for them. May I drop them off to you tomorrow?"

"Yes, Inspector, have you found the murderer of Peter Moore?"

"Yes, sir, we cannot prosecute them as they too have died. I cannot reveal the identity of the person."

"Well done Inspector, at least I can get my diary back."

THIRD PARTY REVIEWS OF PREVIOUS BOOKS

ArtZFriend 5.0 out of 5 stars

Starts Off with a Bang and Will Keep You Up All Night!

Reviewed in the United States on 22 May 2017

Verified Purchase

I read this one in a week because I had some other things going on in my personal life like my gig with Odyssey and my book collection efforts. But to be honest, this one really is a quickie. Alright, let me get right down to my review for you. It started off with a bang. From the first few pages, an old (maybe about in their late fifties to early sixties) couple was just returning from a New Year's Eve Party that they had attended with both of their daughters who decided to stay late with their friends when they nearly collided with a rushing black car coming in the opposite direction but still in their lane. The couple brushed it off and arrived home at their farm that they just bought three years prior. They saw that their dog, Purdy, was fast asleep in their utility room because she had been given a sedative to calm her nerves since she was afraid of the noise made by fireworks that went off when the New Year rang in moments ago. The couple, named Peter and Ann Wall, went straight to bed.

The next day, Peter the husband woke up early to do his usual routine of driving Jumbo, his 1955 Series Two Land Rover to a solitary oak tree that stood on top of a mound that allowed him to view the house and outbuildings. Well, as he drove Jumbo, something happened that got his head cut off and leaving him dead for good on New Year's Day. It was just a few hours later that Ann his wife woke up and went looking for him that she found him beheaded and deceased and changed her and her daughters' lives from then on. Now the mystery in the death was whether Peter had some type of plan to end his life this way or was he killed by someone else. This brought in a slew of characters and unfortunate events that made this book a page-turner during this cold May 2017 for me.

I loved this book. It was the pace I needed for my own personal enjoyment. It did not drag on like some books I read and reviewed. Nope. This book had me reading from beginning to end hungry to find out what could have caused the uncanny death of Peter Wall. The man isn't just anybody. He's the owner of a company that makes a lot of profit and he has a lot of money ready to be bequeathed to his wife and two daughters if in the event that he dies. Insurance I mean. I am glad that I read this novel because it is set in England and Ireland. It is a great glimpse into that part of the world as there are some terms featured and mentioned in it that seem foreign and un-American. There are some places' names that are similar to ones here in the East Coast like Grosvenor and Cheshire. Anyway, to make this review short and simple, I assure you that you will not waste your money on this one if you are looking for a quick read for this upcoming summer season. I guarantee it!

Bookish Kenz 4.0 out of 5 stars

Great prose, great characters and a cracking plot

Reviewed in the United States on 28 May 2017

Verified Purchase

When the head of a wealthy family is found dead on the first day of the new millennium, all the evidence points to suicide. But, can this really be the case when there are some hefty life insurance policies left behind.

Time's Up by R.A. Jordan is a gripping thriller, full of suspense, suspicion, family drama and intrigue. Well-written, with a rapid page-turning plot, I found myself reading 'just one more chapter' many times. Twists and turns in the story will have you constantly questioning what really happened to the patriarch of the Walls. You will wonder about the motives of each family member and work associate, right up to the explosive conclusion. Great prose, great characters and a cracking plot, make for an ideal holiday or lazy weekend read.

All books can be purchased through my website: www.rajordan.uk.

AUTHOR'S COMMENTS

I started to write this little book in 2018, at which time I had the germ of an idea, but I couldn't find a plot to bring the story to an end. I took myself off to Old Trafford on a Stadium Tour of Manchester United's stands and behind the scenes.

So, as I couldn't work out how to take this forward, I set it aside. Since then, I have read Stephen Fry's excellent book *Mythos*. I thank him for all the information, which allowed me to use the exploits of Actaeon. The astute amongst you will have spotted that I don't use the exact spelling for Actaeon in this book. I felt I couldn't use this spelling as numerous companies registered at Companies House use the Stephen Fry spelling. So, I researched and discovered that Cambridge University Classics Department spell the name differently. I have used Aktaion, the Cambridge spelling. There is no company registered with that spelling.

Should it be the case that an organisation operating with the 'Cambridge' spelling, I apologise, but I stress to all readers this book is a work of fiction. All individuals, companies and places are fictitious. The locus of some of the narrative is set in a real place, but again I stress everything that happens is fictitious.

I would like to thank the guide at Manchester United who showed me around in 2018, extremely knowledgeable and informative.

ABOUT THE AUTHOR

I turned to writing in 2009, however, as the other Robert Jordan author, now deceased, wrote Sci-Fi, I decided to use my initials, R A Jordan, to avoid confusion.

On a two-hour delayed train journey from London to Macclesfield there was sufficient time for me to write a plot and synopsis for the first novel, *Time's Up* (Book 1). Another murder and further intrigue is in the second book *England's Wall* and will ensure the pages are turned.

I have attended two creative writing workshops at Oxford University held by the *Sunday Times* during the literary festival. That experience and the love of writing coupled with the 'strange' happenings during the writing of the novels, has propelled me to write five books.

The initial thoughts came as the financial crisis was at 'full bore', giving fuel for the literary fire that was burning inside me (*Laundry*, Book 3). The stories follow the fortunes and misfortunes of the Wall family throughout the first decade of the twenty-first century. Based in Cheshire's county town Chester, the county in which I was born and I know well. The family business of the main characters of the books is civil engineering and latterly property development, activities I myself have been involved with during my forty-five years as a Fellow of the Royal Institution of Chartered Surveyors.

Cracks in the Wall (Book 4) enters a new realm of mystery and intrigue, with abduction of a child and the financial crisis coming together to cause serious problems for the family and the business. An arson attack on the old HQ building of the family firm puts the suspect in jail. It couldn't be Sandra's lover as they were in Spain together – could it?

I have used my experience in property, travel,

sailing, and a love of classic cars to give credence to my plots. The fifth book, *Secret Side*, was published in the first half of 2018.

My next short story *A Family Lie* will be published in 2021. Equally my next novel *A Tower of strength* will be published in 2022. If you wish to be notified of impending releases please register with my mailing list at www.rajordan.uk.

Printed in Great Britain
by Amazon